CAZ REDPATH

Till Death Parts Us

Copyright © 2024 by Caz Redpath

All rights reserved. No part of this publication may be reproduced, stored or transmitted in any form or by any means, electronic, mechanical, photocopying, recording, scanning, or otherwise without written permission from the publisher. It is illegal to copy this book, post it to a website, or distribute it by any other means without permission.

This novel is entirely a work of fiction. The names, characters and incidents portrayed in it are the work of the author's imagination. Any resemblance to actual persons, living or dead, events or localities is entirely coincidental.

Caz Redpath asserts the moral right to be identified as the author of this work.

Editing by Hannah G. Scheffer-Wentz, English Proper Editing Services

First edition

This book was professionally typeset on Reedsy. Find out more at reedsy.com

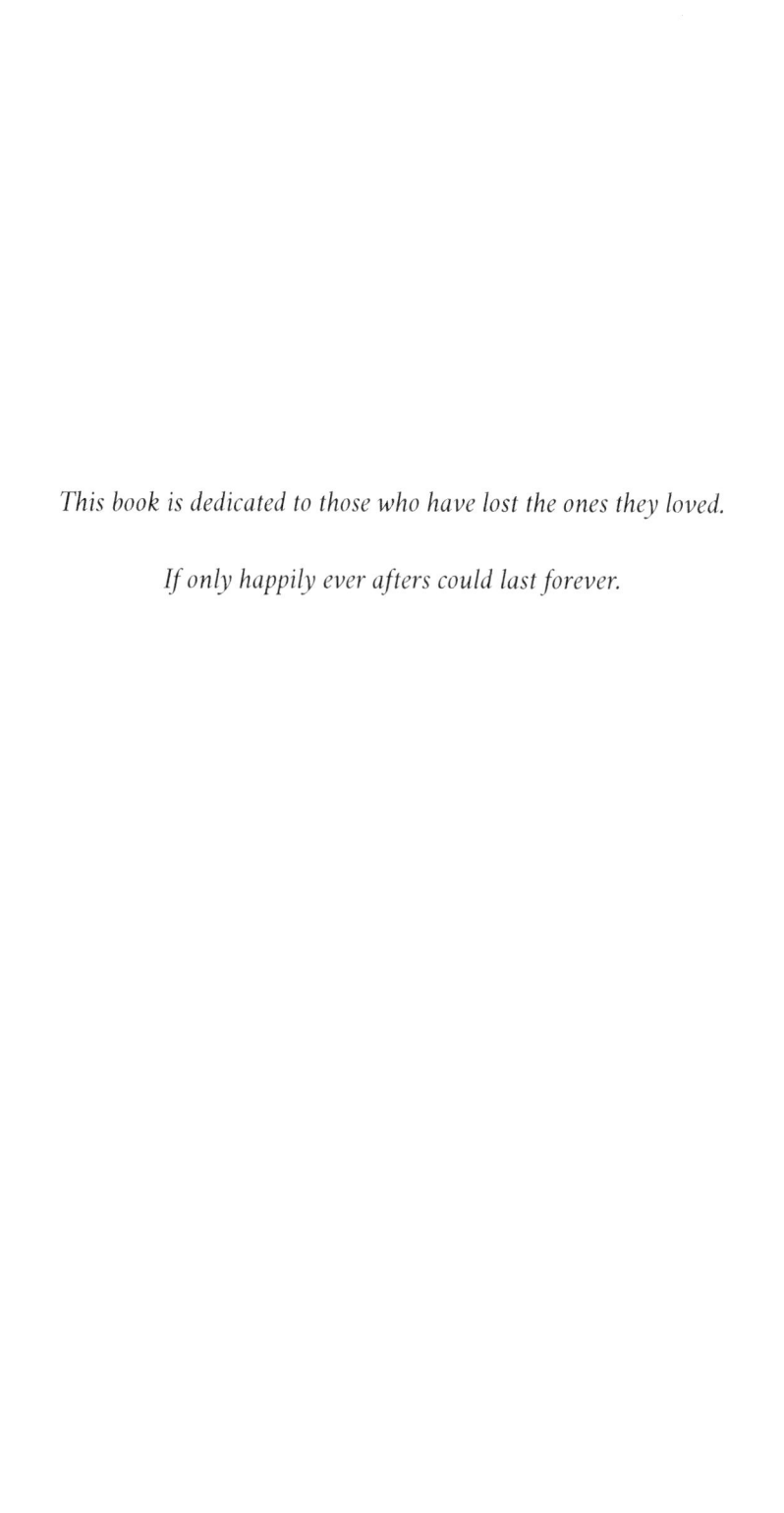

This book is dedicated to those who have lost the ones they loved.

If only happily ever afters could last forever.

"when death
takes my hand
i will hold you with the other
and promise to find you
in every lifetime"

Rupi Kaur

Contents

Preface iv
Content Warnings v
1 Unknown 1
2 Lucy 5
3 James 11
4 Lucy 15
5 James 22
6 Lucy 26
7 James 32
8 Lucy 37
9 James 42
10 Lucy 47
11 James 53
12 Lucy 57
13 James 62
14 Lucy 68
15 James 73
16 Lucy 79
17 James 83
18 Lucy 88
19 James 93
20 Lucy 97
21 James 102
22 Lucy 107

23	James	111
24	Lucy	116
25	James	121
26	Lucy	127
27	James	131
28	Lucy	136
29	James	142
30	Lucy	147
31	James	152
32	Lucy	156
33	James	160
34	Lucy	164
35	James	169
36	Lucy	173
37	James	177
38	Lucy	181
39	James	185
40	Lucy	189
41	James	194
42	Lucy	200
43	James	204
44	Lucy	208
45	James	213
46	Lucy	216
47	James	219
48	Lucy	223
49	James	227
50	Lucy	228
51	James	234
52	Lucy	239
53	James	243

54	Lucy	249
55	James	252
56	Lucy	255
57	James	258
58	Lucy	263
59	James	266
60	Lucy	269
Acknowledgments		274
Also by Caz Redpath		276

Preface

Till Death Parts Us is the second book in The Rosehaven Series. Whilst these books can be read as standalones, below is the recommended reading order:

- Read My Rights
- Till Death Parts Us

Content Warnings

Till Death Parts Us contains references to the following topics:

- Murder and Attempted Murder
- Violence
- Grief
- Loss of a loved one/partner

One

Unknown

Some people deserve to die.

If you had said that to me a week ago, I would have argued this point.

I would tell you maybe people are capable of change, that they can be rehabilitated. That version of me is gone now and in this case, they deserve everything they have coming to them. Truthfully, I don't think death is enough of a punishment, but I don't know if I have it in me to make them suffer. *I'm not a monster.*

I've never killed anyone before but sometimes justice needs to be taken into your own hands.

My eyes wander to the light in the kitchen as I approach the house, their outline coming into view. Washing up dishes seems like such a basic activity, like something any normal person would do. Was it exhausting to have to pretend all the time?

Making my way up to the door, I gently knocked, trying to make the sound of my fist on the door as non-threatening as possible. I don't know why I was so worried since I was an expected guest; my appearance was no surprise. The door swung open and I was greeted with a smile.

"Better late than never." There was a jovial tone to the words and I gave a small chuckle, but I could feel the tension tight in my body. The weight of what I was about to do was heavy on my shoulders.

"Sorry I'm late." I returned the smile as I entered the house. I had been sitting in the car round the corner just trying to convince myself I was doing the right thing. "I did bring your favourite or so I'm told, anyway." I smiled wider as I held up the bottle of malbec in my hand.

"Oh, you know my poison. Red wine has a history of getting me into a lot of trouble over the years." A light chuckle followed. *It was about to again*, I thought to myself. "Can I interest you in a glass?" I shook my head.

"I'm driving, I need to keep a clear head." Besides, I prefer my wine *without* sleeping pills mixed in with it. "Just a soda for me, if you have it." My words were met with a nod as they moved towards the fridge. I watched as they poured my drink and then a glass of wine from the bottle for themselves. My entire body froze as I watched them bring the glass to their lips; I could feel my heart pounding in my chest. Suddenly, I felt panicked that they might be able to taste what I have done. I didn't need them to be completely asleep, I just needed their defences down. A little wooziness to make the whole thing easier.

My eyes wandered around the kitchen.

It was littered with photos, ranging from candid shots to

staged photos. I wondered how it felt to live a lie, to hide who you truly were from all those that knew you. I can't even imagine waking up and finding out everything you know about the person you cared for was wrong. That the person you loved was a monster.

I guess if this didn't go my way, then people would be wondering that about me tomorrow. People I know waking up to the news that I killed someone. Details of my crimes plastered all over the newspaper. My family weeping in the living room as a police officer is telling them that the person they knew was capable of heinous, wicked crimes. I hope it didn't come to that. I had worked out this plan in detail.

This was going to work.

Even if I got caught, I wouldn't be sorry. There would be no regret in my expression as I was dragged down to the station. Murder is evil, but sometimes it is necessary. The world will be a lot safer without them, I was certain of that. It was what encouraged me to be brave.

I struggled to take my eyes away from the photos as polite conversation continued. The usual talks about the weather and work ensued for a while. I turned my head, eyes now on the glass as more was poured. This was going to be easier than expected if they kept drinking like that.

"I'm thinking of trying that new restaurant downtown this week. Decent food has been missing from my life for a while." If only they knew they wouldn't be making that trip.

This almost felt cruel—even death row inmates got a last meal. Maybe I should have brought something.

"It's supposed to be excellent," they continued. The slight slur on the last word caught my attention. *It's time.*

"Did I tell you about—"

"We need to talk." My voice was harsh as I interrupted.

"Is that not exactly what we are doing?" I could hear the tension in their voice, the smile falling straight from their face.

"I know *everything*." There was a silence as our eyes met, an understanding happening between us as to what everything was. "You thought you'd be able to hide it from me?" A bitterness clouded my tone. I stood from my seat and walked towards the counter where they were leaning.

"It was an accident." The shake in their tone surprised me. I was expecting more confidence in their crimes. Maybe I was more intimidating than I realised.

"It wasn't an accident and you know it. What about all the others?" I spat. "I can't let you hurt anyone else." Their eyes widened, panic creeping in. Before I allowed them to respond, I launched myself towards them, pressing them to the floor with my hands around their throat. There were attempts at thrashing, attempts to push me off them, but they were futile. For once in my life, I felt like I had the upper hand. Slowly, their fight faded and I watched as their whole body went still underneath me. I waited a moment to be sure before moving myself off of them. I took a deep breath as I stood up and looked at what I had done.

My emotions were conflicted. On one hand, I know I have just saved more people from getting hurt by their hands. On the other hand, I have just made myself no better than them.

Some people deserved to die, I reminded myself.

Two

Lucy

My father is a killer.

I try to listen to the officer in front of me, but I can't stop the room from spinning. He is keeping the details light, the word *alleged* dangles in the air, but there is a hesitation each time he says it. He doesn't believe his own words, I can tell. He wants to say that my father is a murderer, he doesn't think for one second he is innocent. I am torn between wishing he would fill me in on every single detail of my father's *alleged* crime and wanting to put my hands over my ears to block out his words. I feel a scream building inside my chest, desperate to be let out, but I hold it in. *Is the air getting thin in here?*

"Mrs. Davis," he addresses my mother directly. "It is still an ongoing investigation, so I am unable to give much detail, but a young woman was strangled in her home." He says the words *ongoing investigation* for what must be the tenth time.

Anger threatens to pour out of me, but I have a rein on it. This isn't the officer's fault. He looks just as anxious to leave this room as I am. It can't be easy to be the one who has to deliver bad news. To know you are about to shatter someone's whole world.

My mother clutches my hand sobbing, repeating *I knew it*, over and over. I want to point out to her that if she knew it, why were they married for twenty-five years? Surely, you didn't want to admit you knew you married a killer? I don't point this out, obviously; that would be cruel, but her words do nothing to ease the tension in this living room. My mother always had a flare for the dramatics.

My eyes catch sight of a family photo on the mantelpiece. My mother and father are smiling back at me, a younger version of myself on his shoulders. The mood of the photo is a far cry from the mood in this room. We are happy there, my smile wide as I sit on the shoulders of a monster. *Allegedly*.

I zoned back in as the police officer told us due to the severity of the crimes, my father would not make bail. We wouldn't have had the money to bail him out, even if we had wanted to. Our family wasn't exactly in the strongest financial position. My father worked two jobs, one at a grocery store and the other doing night cleans at our local high school. My mother didn't work; she was a stay-at-home mother still, despite the fact I'm in college and hadn't needed taking care of for years. So, my father had to work twice as hard. He never complained, though, even on the nights where he barely got a couple hours of sleep. He did everything he could to keep a roof over our heads.

I thought of him now, his arrest. I tried to picture him committing the crime he was accused of, but I couldn't marry up the versions of my father. The man who worked so hard for us, who always cared for us, killed a woman in cold blood? It just didn't make sense. Did they catch him in the act? When they cuffed him, were his hands shaking or was he not affected by the actions? I shivered at the thought.

He had left for work this morning as normal. Is that where they arrested him? I imagined them dragging him down to the station, his hands cuffed tightly. If he was a killer, they wouldn't exactly be treating him nicely. He would be stripped of his clothes, taken to jail, and put into an orange jumpsuit. Orange was *not* his colour. Although, I guess that wouldn't be at the forefront of his mind right now.

Was my father *really* a killer? He had never once in my life hurt me. Surely someone with the ability to kill would have been an abuser at home, too. Didn't killers usually start off by hurting animals? He loved our dog, Cato. Sometimes I thought he loved him more than me. He had never touched my mother either, at least not that I had ever seen. He was the kind of man who brought her flowers on a Friday and always told her he loved her before he went to work.

The police officer may have been sparse on the details, but we knew the victim was a woman which only led to further questions. *Was he having an affair?* I couldn't imagine my father ever cheating on my mother, but I also never would have imagined him as a killer, either. Maybe there are a lot of things I don't know about him. My eyes found that picture again—he looked like a stranger to me now.

I had realised that I was already classing him as guilty in my head. I didn't know that for sure, there was still a chance he was innocent. Maybe they got the wrong man and this would all blow over by the morning. He was an *alleged* killer,

Till Death Parts Us

I reminded myself. I wanted to believe he was innocent; I *needed* to believe he was innocent.

The officer's eyes when he spoke about my father filled my head with doubts. I wanted to beg him to tell me the truth. To tell me what he really thought about this situation. To stop playing devil's advocate. To stop using that word, *alleged,* if he didn't really mean it.

"Lucy," my mother said in a tone that made it clear this was not the first time she had attempted to get my attention. "Officer Harris wants to know if you have any questions." *I had more questions than I knew what to do with.* None of which I thought Officer Harris would be able to answer me right now. I shook my head softly.

"I have a question," my mother said, releasing my hand. "When will we know more details about what Anthony did?"

The thought made me feel sick. I was not sure if I was ready to hear what my father had done. *Allegedly.* I didn't want to hear or read about him brutally murdering someone on the radio or in the paper.

Oh my God, this was going to be headline news tomorrow.

Everyone in Kirkston City was going to know my father was being accused of murder. What if it hits national news? How was I supposed to show up to college on Monday with *Anthony Davis kills young woman* plastered everywhere?

I could see it now, everyone's eyes watching me as I walked down the hallway.

Knowing that I was the daughter of a monster. The few friends I had would distance themselves from me. If I was in their position, would I do the same? The phrase *innocent until proven guilty* came to mind. People didn't seem to wait for that judgement.

Lucy

I desperately searched through my memories for signs that I missed, signs that I should have seen this all coming. I couldn't think of a single one. I had no warning that any of this was coming. I felt so stupid and naïve.

"As soon as we know more, we will contact you, I believe they are interviewing your husband as we speak."

I wondered how my dad was feeling. I could only envisage how terrified he must be. Trying to hold it together whilst the police asked him every question under the sun. He wouldn't be getting any sleep tonight and I doubt I would, either. I wasn't sure if I'd ever be able to fall asleep again with the images running through my mind.

"Can we see him?" I asked. My mother shot me a glance, the hatred evident in her eyes.

"Why would you want to see him?" she spat. I felt tears welling up in my eyes, but I fought them off. I didn't *want* to see him, I *needed* to see him. I needed to know for myself if he was innocent. If I could talk to him, ask him questions, then I would know. I would know if I was looking at a monster or not. I was sure of it. Despite everything, he was still my father and I needed to know he was okay.

"You won't be able to see him today, but we may be able to let you see him tomorrow," Officer Harris said, ignoring my mother's question. I felt my mother's gaze burn through me as I thanked Officer Harris for his answer. My father was gone and I could already sense my mother pulling away from me.

"I have everything I need for now and the officers have finished looking around the house," he said, clearly desperate to get away from the tense atmosphere that filled the room. He probably has a nice, not fucked up family to go home to. "But we will need you both to come down to the station tomorrow to answer questions about Anthony." We both nodded quietly. I knew it was obvious they would want to talk to us about him. Did they think we had anything to do with it? No, we would be in handcuffs, too, if they did. I was grateful to at least not have to face their questions until the morning. I needed time to process.

My mother thanked Officer Harris and led him out to the front door. I left the sitting room and made my way upstairs to my bedroom. I felt like I couldn't breathe down there. I shut the door and my resolve crumbled as I slid to the floor, the sobs breaking their way out of me as I held my knees close to my chest.

My father was a killer.

Allegedly, I reminded myself.

I desperately clung to that word; it was my last hope. He had to be innocent. He just had to be.

But what if he wasn't?

Is the ability to kill genetic? Was I suddenly going to turn into a deranged killer, too? Have I been a monster this whole time?

People always told me I was just like my father. I used to love being likened to him, but now the thought terrified me.

I needed to see him.

Three

James

Grab me a coffee, James.
File this away for me, James.
Deliver this to the other side of town after hours, James.
Bend to my every command, won't you, James.

You wouldn't believe me if I told you I loved my job, would you? Working as a criminal defence lawyer has been a dream of my entire life. I was fascinated with crime and statistics. I always wanted to defend those who deserved it, those who didn't have anyone else looking out for them. When I saw this job advertised just after I graduated, I jumped at it. I had thought working for a smaller company that does pro-bono cases that I would miss out on having to do the lackey work.

I was mistaken.

Sawyer's Law Firm only took on a handful of cases and they only took on cases where they believed the accused was innocent. We had limited resources and didn't have the time to waste on those who were clearly guilty. It was part of my job to phone the rejected cases and let them know we wouldn't be taking them on. I was grateful when I got the answering machine.

"James!" The loud voice of my boss, Michael Sawyer, boomed from the other room. Like a good boy, I walked quickly over to him.

"Jam—"he began to shout again as I entered the room before he caught sight of me. "There you are, I need you to do another coffee run for the whole office. We are all going to be working late tonight on the Jake Murray case." He dismissed me with a wave. His words didn't require a response; this was an order, not a question. I shuffled out of the room, taking coffee orders as I went around the office.

The Murray case was the biggest case the firm had gotten since I worked here. He was an ordinary mailman who had been accused of murdering the son of a high member in one of the biggest gangs in Kirkston City. It was obvious to anyone that he had been set up by a rival gang, but the evidence against him was damning. It was all planted evidence, of course.

Knowing in your heart someone was innocent was one thing, proving it was another. I prided myself in my ability to tell when someone was lying, but it wasn't always enough.

I would give anything to shadow Michael on this case. I'd wipe his ass if I had to. Outside the courtroom Michael was an asshole, but inside? He was a mastermind. He captivated juries, had them wrapped around his finger in just his opening statements. The coverage of this case would be huge and I knew Michael would give it everything he got. I needed to be in that courtroom with him. If I became half the lawyer he was, it would be an incredible achievement. My career was everything to me; I'd worked so hard to get to this point. It was the most important thing in my life.

As much as I hated being the lackey of the office, it had some perks. There was bright sunshine outside today, so I took the walk to the coffee shop slowly. I'd be balancing far more coffees than one man should carry on the way back, so I could at least enjoy the nice weather on the way there.

Days like this made me miss home.

My hometown of Rosehaven was only an hour away, but I hardly seemed to get the time to visit. I looked around as I walked—everyone always seemed to be in a rush. The sound of cars honking filled the air. I never heard the quiet anymore, even in my apartment there was always noise. People outside, neighbours yelling at each other, and somebody's dog barking were constant noises in my ears. I missed the quiet. I missed going to the lake with my friends, taking a little boat out and fishing. I missed running along the trails, feeling the wind through me. *I missed my home.*

I moved away for college and stayed for the job. I don't regret the move; I'm building my career and I'm doing important work. Besides, I am only twenty-two. I have an abundance of years ahead of me to live the quiet life.

Maybe I could go back home or live in another small town with a wife and kids someday. Maybe one day we'd retire together, drive a little RV across the country as we lived out our final years.

I couldn't allow myself to focus on these maybes now; my father always drilled in the importance of building up the career first.

I often felt the weight of my parents on my shoulders. When

I was fifteen, my older sister and I got into a car crash. A drunk driver ran a red light straight into the driver's side of the car. My older sister, Alice, was driving and didn't make it. I am all my parents have left now. I feel this immense pressure to be the best at everything, like me being successful in life would make up for the fact she isn't here.

It doesn't.

My sister was everything I wished I could be, in both the academic sense and in the social sense. She was kind, she was patient, and she always did whatever she could to help others. Often, I felt survivor's guilt. I got away from that crash with nothing more than a broken leg and some bruises. It took me a long time to fully recover physically, but I'm still here.

My parents and I were not as close as you'd think we would be, given the situation. They rarely ever called and when they did, they only wanted to know about work. Sometimes, I wished they saw me as more than my achievements.

Alice was everything I am not and she is the one who should still be here. Here I am moaning about having to do a coffee run while she would do it with grace. I let the sun shine down on my face for another moment before I entered the coffee shop.

Alice being gone was a reminder to me that I needed to live, life was short. So what if I had to do lackey work until I earned my place within the law firm? I was still here; it was important to be grateful for every moment.

Some people were having a far worse time than I was right now.

Four

Lucy

Sleep eluded me just as I thought it would. Cato had snuck into bed with me during the night, it was like he sensed I needed comfort. *We didn't deserve dogs.*

I couldn't help but stare at my ceiling and wonder where everything had gone wrong.

I replayed every memory of my father that I could think of, trying to find moments that made this all make sense. They weren't there. I could not make sense in my mind that this man, my father, was a killer. It had been twelve hours since we found out the news, but I felt like I could barely remember the time before everything fell apart. Was it only yesterday when we all sat and had breakfast together?

As each minute passed, I found myself getting more and more desperate to see him. I had more questions that I knew what to do with and no answers.

My mother and I didn't speak again after the officer left, I shut myself in my room and ignored her soft knocks on the door. She had written my father off the second the officer told her of his crimes. Admittedly, initially, I did too, but now I'm not so sure. I still cling to that hope that he is innocent. If she wasn't going to fight for him, then I would. How could her love for him fade so quickly?

Reluctantly, I removed myself from the bed and started to get dressed. We hadn't been given an official time to go to the station, just in the morning. I could hear my mother clanging around in the kitchen downstairs. I imagine sleep eluded her, too. Bracing myself, I opened the door and made my way in the kitchen. My mother's head snapped up to look at me as I entered. For a moment, we were silent. What was there to say? Her exhaustion was painted over her face as I am sure mine was, too.

I wanted to feel angry with her about how quickly she threw away any hope of my father being innocent. I spent all night raging about it, but now as I stood in front of her, that anger faded. I saw a fragile and vulnerable woman in front of me. Just as I had thought my father loved me, she had thought he loved her. Her entire marriage was in shambles and I hid in my room like a coward. I moved towards her and wrapped my arms around her. We embraced quietly for a moment before the tears began to fall. I could feel her sobs against me as I let mine go. Both of our hearts had been broken and now we needed to find a way to piece them back together. This was not the time to fall apart from each other.

"I'm sorry," I whispered softly as I tried to fight a second wave of tears. I felt her shake her head against me.

"There is nothing for you to be sorry for, it is *him* who should be sorry." Her voice was stern as she started to pull herself together. We moved away from each other, a heaviness in my chest still that I didn't know how to rid myself of.

"We should eat some breakfast," she said as she clapped her hands together. "We eat, we pull ourselves together, and we go down to that police station." She was right, of course. My mother was always a stricter parent than my father. He was soft on me, always letting me get away with things. This is why this whole thing seems backwards.

"I still want to talk to him." I watched her eyes cloud over as I spoke, shaking her head softly.

"I won't stop you," she sighed. "But I won't join you, either." I'd convinced myself that if I saw him, I would be able to rid myself of the heaviness in my chest. That I would know one way or the other if the man sat before me was a monster.

If he wasn't, then I would do everything I could to help him prove his innocence.

If he was guilty, then today would be the last day I saw him. The weight of that clung to me.

It would hurt to never see him again. He deserved whatever punishment he got if he was guilty.

His trial may not have started, but today was judgement day for my father. In my eyes at least.

Our breakfast together was silent. I pushed the food around my plate, but honestly, I could barely even stomach a few bites. My mother eventually gave up on her own uneaten breakfast and went upstairs to change. For a few moments, I was left alone with my thoughts. I felt like I was stuck on a broken cycle, just replaying everything. I was relieved when my mother came back down the stairs and we headed out to the car.

"You will need to be honest about everything," she said softly.

I couldn't help but tilt my head in confusion.

"What do you mean?" I questioned.

"You need to tell the truth about everything, no matter what they ask." I tried to work out what she was referring to. The honest truth was that I didn't see any of this coming, and despite her constant repetition of the words, *I knew it*, yesterday. I don't believe she knew it was coming, either. I didn't respond, instead focusing my attention out the window of the car digesting her words. They made me feel that there was more to this situation and my father than I was aware of. I wondered what she was going to say when the police spoke to her. I had hoped she would change her mind about seeing my father. I was nervous about seeing him on my own. Before I could get a chance to think too much about it, we were at the station. We were both silent as we exited the car and headed into the building.

"We are relatives of Anthony Davis," my mother said as we approached the front desk. "We were asked to come in to make statements and answer some questions." I could hear the shame in her voice as she spoke. The officer behind the desk looked up, I watched his expression as he scanned the two of us. He looked disgusted, like the idea he was looking at two people related to Anthony Davis was horrific.

"Sit down in the waiting room and an officer will come get you and take you through." If his words could shoot venom, that tone would have been a fatal shot. We had barely touched the seat when a suited man walked out.

"Lucy Davis?" His eyes wandered the room before they met mine. "Come with me, please." I looked at my mother. I guess it made sense we would be interviewed separately, but I still wasn't prepared for this moment. Cautiously, I followed the man into a cold looking room with just a table and chairs. The light in this room felt brighter than I had ever seen before and suddenly my mouth was dry. He motioned for me to sit and I did, still trying to search around the room, hoping to spot something that would make me feel better. I didn't, the only thing I felt was fear.

"My name is Detective Mason," he began. I looked at the table. I couldn't bear to look in his eyes. If he looked at me like the man at the front desk, I might throw up. "I need to ask you some questions about your father, get a bit of background into your family, if that's okay." I nodded; I still hadn't found my voice.

"What was your childhood like?" His voice was soft and it only seemed to unnerve me more. I was expecting anger—being met with kindness made me feel uneasy.

"Fairly normal." There was a crack in my voice as I spoke. "Happy," I added.

"Your dad was a good father?" I thought about this for a second before answering. The answer was *yes,* I knew that without thinking, but I was wondering how to portray it in a way to make him understand.

"He is a *great* dad." It was the truth, never for one moment did my father not make me feel loved. "He doted on us all the time." My eyes finally looked up as I met the detective's.

"Did he hit you?" he asked, his stare hardening. The question took me by surprise initially. He was trying to get a read on me to see if I was lying.

"No, he's never hit me."

"Did he hit your mother?" His eyes looked determined, like he desperately wanted to find something here.

"Never," I fired back.

"Are you sure? You know what he has been accused of, don't you?" His voice was patronising now, gone was the softness from when he first spoke. "He strangled a woman to death in her own home."

"*Allegedly,*" I reminded him. I suddenly felt protective of my father. The man who had always looked after me now needed me to look after him. He needed me in his corner.

"Allegedly," he confirmed. "He *allegedly* went to this woman's house on a date, gave her sleeping pills in her wine to overpower her, and strangled her to death in her kitchen." He moved a photo closer to me and suddenly I felt my entire breakfast threatening to come back. In front of me was a picture of a woman lifeless on the floor, a smashed wine glass by her side, and bruises on her neck. I felt my whole body begin to shake as I leant back in the chair trying to cover my eyes.

"I'll ask you again. Has he ever hit you or your mother?" His voice was stern. I took what felt like hours, but must have only been a few minutes, to respond as I tried to calm myself down from what I just saw.

"He *never* touched us." I tried to have confidence in my answer, but my whole world was shaking around me, everything crumbling right before my eyes. The detective continued to badger me with questions about my father, his whereabouts that night and our life, all the while that photo laid on the table. The woman was a pretty blonde, barely a couple of years older than myself. The thought of my father having an affair with a woman so close to my age brought another level of pain and confusion to the mix. Her entire life, gone at the hands of another, allegedly at the hands of my father. She had so much life to live and now she would never

Lucy

get a chance to live any of it.

My father's fingerprints were all over this lady's house as well as on one of the wine glasses. There was no sign of forced entry, according to Detective Mason. There was no sign of anyone else having been there but the two of them. Everything pointed to my father. He used the words *open and shut case* several times.

The whole time the detective spoke, there was one thought that kept popping into my head. This woman was small, fragile looking. My father was a large man, over six feet tall. Why did he need to give her sleeping pills to overpower her? Surely, he would have easily been able to overpower her even if she was completely sober? It didn't make sense.

My mothers word filled my head. *You need to tell them about everything.*

They still confused me; I couldn't think of anything else I needed to tell. *Why did it feel like I was missing something?*

After the detective was finally done grilling me, I let out a deep breath. I never wanted to step foot in this room again. Our eyes met once more as I asked,

"Can I see him now?"

Five

James

"All work and no play is making you a boring man, James Weatherston," my friend, Daines, said on the other end of the phone. His name was Jack, but we had two Jacks in our friend group and Daines just sort of stuck. Daines had been my best friend since we were in first grade. I could always count on him to tell me things straight.

"This is a really important point in my career, I can't screw this up." I held the phone with one hand to my ear, twirling the wire with my other.

"You're not going to screw everything up by going out and having fun. It's okay to let loose once in a while. Why don't you come home for a weekend? We can go out and you can *finally* meet Angie."

Angie was the girl Daines was absolutely obsessed with; I'd never heard him talk about a girl the way he did Angie. I was happy for him, but we were at different places in our lives. He had finished up his training at the police academy and was working as an officer in our hometown of Rosehaven. I was out here in the city, trying to build my career and help prove the innocence of those who deserved it.

We had always bonded over our desire to always do what is right.

"You're really serious about her, aren't you?" I asked. I couldn't help but feel a slight pang of jealousy. I wasn't exactly looking for a partner, I was too focused on my career. That didn't mean I wasn't lonely sometimes, though.

"Deadly. You mark my words, James, I will have married this woman by the end of '92." I met his words with a laugh.

"Daines, that's only eighteen months away. You seriously think you're going to be married by then? We're still young, what is the rush?"

"I'd marry her now if I had the money. I want to make sure I get a nice apartment or something set up before I ask her. I am trying to pick up as many shifts as possible to make that happen. She deserves the best."

"You're a sap, you know that?"

"When you find that person, James, you will be a sappy asshole, too. I love her, James. That means something." I hadn't heard him say he loved her before, but hearing it made me smile. I would tease him relentlessly, but he meant the world to me. He was like my brother and I wanted nothing but the best for him.

"I am not exactly in a place to be finding that person right now."

"Why not?"

"I have my career to build."

"Why can't you do both? The two aren't mutually exclusive.

Stop holding up your entire life for this job, James. The years aren't promised, stop waiting for the future to do things you want." His voice was soft, but there was a sternness to this tone. I guess I did have a tendency to focus on the future rather than the present, but the future was what I was building.

"I need to focus; I can't let anything distract me. I'm hoping Michael will pick me to go to court with him for the Murray case."

"The mailman?" It didn't surprise me at all that Daines knew about it—we had shared interests in things like these. "Do you think Michael will get him off?"

"I think Michael is probably his best shot," I answered honestly. I really didn't know if we would be able to prove his innocence, but we would work hard to do it. "Speaking of, I need to go through some case files before I go to bed." I heard Daines groan loudly on the other end of the phone.

"You work too hard," he said with a sigh. "Come back home to visit soon, buddy, I miss you."

"I promise I will. I miss you, too, I'm looking forward to meeting Angie."

"You'll love her." I could hear the smile in his voice. We said our goodbyes and I placed the phone back in its holder.

My apartment wasn't exactly much to write home about. It was a one bed, if you could call that cupboard a bedroom. It was functional and that was all I needed it to be. I found my way to the kitchen, hoping I still had a frozen meal leftover. To my joy, there was a frozen pizza still in the bottom drawer. Chucking it in the cooker, I looked over at the files on the table. I was supposed to go through these and present Michael with anything useful at the Monday meeting. I had already worked four hours later than normal at the office and my brain was

James

fried. Maybe Daines was right, I was working too hard.

I needed to help Jake Murray walk free. He needed me. If I didn't spend time on the case, he could be stuck in jail for the rest of his life for something he didn't do. The work I was doing was important, that is why I can't allow myself to be distracted. I had enough time to have fun and maybe find a girl of my own in the future, but it wasn't a priority for me right now.

The most important thing in my life now was my work and helping those in need. I really didn't see that there would ever be anything more important than that.

The sound of the timer beeping took me out of my thoughts. After plating it up, I sat on the table opening the first file. I only hoped I could get to bed before the early hours of tomorrow. I had a feeling I'd been spending my entire weekend on this.

Six

Lucy

I felt like my heart was going to pound out of my chest as I sat waiting for them to bring my dad into the room. I was starting to feel like asking to see him was a bad idea. *Maybe this was all a mistake.* It probably wasn't too late to tell that detective I changed my mind.

Just as I rose out of my seat, the door opened. I heard the clinking of the handcuffs before I saw him. A police officer led my father into the room with Detective Mason following close behind. I barely took notice of the other two men as my eyes fell on my father and his on mine. His face was covered in bruises, his feet dragging behind him. He hardly seemed to have the energy to put one foot in front of the other. My father was broken.

"Lou…" His voice was breathless as he spoke. I could see the tears threatening to fall in his eyes as he looked at me.

"Dad…" My own voice was shaky as he sat opposite me. He

Lucy

tried to reach out his cuffed hands towards me, but Detective Mason pulled him back forcibly. It was obvious to me they weren't exactly treating him kindly. "What happened to your face?" He didn't say anything at first in return, his eyes looking around the room.

"I fell," he finally said. *We both knew it was a lie.*

"You have five minutes," Detective Mason said as he stepped towards the back of the room. I guess I shouldn't be surprised he wasn't going to leave us alone to talk. Now that I was here, I had no idea what to say, what question to ask first. My thoughts span in my head, making the room spin with it.

"I didn't kill her, Lou," my father spoke first, breaking the silence. I tried to analyse his expression, trying to decipher if he was lying. I thought I would know instantly if he was guilty or not, but now that I was in the room with him? I was just as confused as before. "I swear to you, I didn't kill her."

"Then why do they think it was you?" I asked, finally finding my voice.

"I knew her, Amber." He paused. I hadn't heard her name before. *Amber.* That name was going to haunt me for the rest of my life, I could feel it.

"How did you know her?" I asked, sensing his hesitation.

"We were…" he paused again, "romantically involved." A wave of nausea swept through me.

"So you were fucking her?" Detective Mason cleared his throat awkwardly.

"Lou, you do not use that language," my father said sternly, as if he still had the right to parent me.

"I don't think you have the right to tell me what I can and can't do in this moment, do you, Dad?" My voice was harsh, I didn't have the patience. This was a *mistake.*

"We were sleeping together, yes," he sighed. "We've been seeing each other for the past couple of weeks." His words made me feel sick. The thought of him sneaking out behind my mother's back to see this woman. How could he even show his face in our home after what he had done? How did he go out, sleep with this woman, and then come home and tell my mother he loved her? A woman that only looked to be a few years older than his daughter? Maybe he *was* a monster, especially since he was able to hide this from us. Even if he was innocent of her murder, there was still plenty to repent for.

I was angry, so angry I couldn't speak for a few moments. I glared at him, fury almost choking me.

"You killed her, didn't you?" I replied sharply. The thought made me shudder. All I could picture was his hands around her throat, pinning her down. *But why did he drug her?* The question floated in my head again. Maybe there was no sense to his actions.

"Lou, no. I would never." His voice was desperate. "You know I wouldn't do that."

"I don't know what to believe any more." A look of tired sadness passed over his features as I spoke. Yesterday morning, I believed my father was one of the greatest men that I knew, that he loved me and my mother with everything he had. Everything he was to me is shattered on the floor.

"Is this the first time you've cheated on Mom?" I asked, watching as he swallowed hard. His face told me all I needed to know. Amber wasn't the first, clearly far from it.

"Your mother and I haven't been happy for a while," he said, as if this fact was obvious. From where I was sitting, they were desperately in love. I didn't think for a second that they

Lucy

weren't happy in their marriage. I could feel a sense of sadness begin to overwhelm me as I started playing with my hands in my lap. I felt his eyes narrowed on me. I wondered if he looked her in the eye when he killed her.

"Why did you drug her?" I realised my line of questions was insinuating guilt. My anger was clouding my ability to remain impartial.

"I didn't." His face fell into his hand. "I *loved* her, Lucy." He paused and I felt tears well in my eyes. Yesterday, I had no idea who this woman was and now, not only had I found out how she had been killed, I found out my father was in love with her. He didn't love my mother, he loved *her*. I was scared of what else I didn't know. "I would never hurt her. I don't know who hurt her, but if I ever find them, I—" He cut himself off, looking awkwardly behind him. He had clearly forgotten the detective was still in the room. Of the situation that we are currently in. I could see the swift shadow of anger sweep across his face. "I loved her," he repeated as tears started to fall down his face.

I had never seen my father cry. It made me feel uneasy to watch him show vulnerability in this way. Our parents were always meant to be the ones who were strong for us, who protected us. Yet here I am, watching my father break down into sobs before me. Tears started to fall down my own face. He was heartbroken, that much was obvious.

"I don't think you killed her." The words were out of my mouth before I could stop them. It was the truth, watching him now. Seeing the way he sobbed for her. For another woman who isn't in our family. I don't think he did it, I truly believe my father is innocent.

"What can I do to help?"

He was quiet for a moment, clearly trying to gather himself. "I need a lawyer." He cleared his throat. "We can't afford one, but there are firms that take on pro-bono cases. I need you to contact them for me and hopefully they can help me. Help prove that I am innocent." He turned to the detective briefly before his attention came back to me. "One of the officers said they have leaflets at the front desk, numbers you can call."

I nodded. "I'll call them, I promise." For a moment, I saw a brief smile on his lips and I met it with a small smile. I realised I was probably the first person who had believed him since his arrest.

"Where were you when she was murdered?" This was the final test for me, to help me decide if he really was innocent.

"I did see Amber that night," he confesses. "I had an early start the next day, so we had dinner and then I left," he sighed. "I should have stayed, maybe then she would still be here." He sniffed as he rubbed his hands over his face. "I should have stayed with her."

I watched his face intently as he spoke. Call me naïve, but he seemed like he meant every word. I could hear the regret in his voice when he said he should have stayed. As if that decision was going to haunt him for the rest of his life, like he blamed himself.

"Time's up," Detective Mason said bluntly.

He wasn't exactly keeping his cards close to his chest as hatred filled his eyes. He grabbed hold of my father, pulling him from his seat with unnecessary force.

"I love you, Lou," my father said as he was dragged from the room.

"I love you. I'll get you a lawyer, I promise," I called after him as I watched him disappear down the corridor.

Lucy

My father was innocent. I knew that now and I was going to do whatever it took to free him. I don't think calling was going to be enough, I would knock doors down until someone helped him. I would do whatever it took.

Seven

James

I wasted my entire weekend looking through those files. I spent the whole time at my kitchen table, looking through them bit by bit. Instead of coming into work refreshed after a peaceful weekend, I was exhausted and truthfully, a little braindead. However, I did come across some info that I intended to present to Michael this morning. A few people reported seeing Murray making rounds at a different part of town to the murder. He would have been hard pushed to have made it from there to murder the victim in the time frame. It wasn't impossible, but it was highly unlikely. If we could get some more statements, some more people to testify he was somewhere else, then there was a chance he would be a free man at the end of this.

Despite my exhaustion, I arrived to work early, buzzing for my presentation in the morning meeting. I hoped this information would secure my seat next to Michael in the courtroom. I was nervous—Michael Sawyer was a hard man to read. In the courtroom you wanted a lawyer with a good poker face, one who didn't make it obvious that they thought they were winning or losing. For clients, their lawyers sometimes quite literally had their life in their hands, they didn't need one who made it obvious when things were going wrong. They needed someone who was going to be strong for them.

I was still working on my poker face, sometimes my reactions gave me away. My father had always said I was a little soft. I didn't regret being soft, but I wanted to be able to shield my emotions when I needed to. If I was going to make it as a lawyer, I needed to learn how to be strong for my clients.

This morning's meeting was good practice for that, I needed to keep my poker face. There was every chance Michael could sit there and laugh at my proposal. If that was the case, I couldn't let him see that he crushed me.

"What have you got for us, Weatherston?" he asked expectantly and I suddenly felt all eyes on me. We were all dying for that seat, everyone wanted to be in the room when it all went down.

"Witness statements," I said, clearing my throat. "They put Jake on the other side of town twenty minutes before the murder. At that time of day, it would take him twenty-five minutes to get to the murder scene in my estimation. Now, I know they could argue that traffic may have been lighter that day, but if we can get some more statements closer to the time of the murder, this could be our chance."

It wouldn't be easy; the gang had threatened most of the locals if they came forward with statements. We were lucky to get the statements we had, but I was willing to knock on those doors myself every day if that is what it took.

Silence filled the room as we waited for Michael to give a reaction. I could feel the hairs on the back of my neck standing up in anticipation.

"Good job, James." He smiled softly. "I don't know how much luck we will get, but it's worth a shot. I'll leave you to organise the walk rounds. Keep digging."

I let out a breath, relieved he wasn't laughing in my face. I was also grateful that my turn to speak was over and I could sit down. We all talked over the case more as well as a handful of others and shared ideas. Not all cases were as big as Murrays, we did a lot of small claims type cases. Usually, I didn't mind those types of cases, I wanted people to have the justice they deserved. Right now, though, my mind was focused on one thing and I wasn't going to let anything distract me from it.

As we all started to file out of the room, the receptionist, Sandra, was heading towards us with a young woman in tow. It was her eyes I first noticed, a bright blue, the kind that I imagined sparkled when she smiled. Although now, she wasn't smiling and a sadness filled those eyes. I found my own drawn to them.

I took in her face next; exhaustion was evident all over it. There was no denying she was beautiful, but it was not what I was focused on. I was focused on how worn down she was. I felt this want to reach out to her, to help her.

"Mr. Sawyer, Lucy Davis is here to see you." Sandra smiled softly.

"Of course, come in." He pointed towards the door. As she walked past me, our eyes met and I offered a soft smile which she returned. *Davis.* I'm sure I'd heard that name before.

James

Anthony Davis. I'd read about him in the paper this morning, he was arrested for the murder of Amber Jones. A young woman who was found strangled and drugged in her home, apparently the two were in a relationship.

Judging by the age of Lucy, she was his daughter. I couldn't even begin to fathom how it felt to be in her shoes. No wonder she looked so vulnerable and exhausted. I imagined she was here to ask for Michael's help. With the Murray case, I wasn't sure he would take it. God, I hoped he was handling this with kindness. The poor girl had been through enough.

They were in that room for barely a few minutes, I watched from my desk the entire time. I couldn't concentrate knowing she was likely getting her heart torn further to pieces in there. As the door opened, Michael leads out with Lucy close behind, tears brimming her eyes.

"Please," she pleaded. "You're the last one on the list." The pain in her voice made my heart shatter as I slowly got to my feet. The entire office was focused on them. It was a show no one could turn themselves away from.

"I'm sorry, but I told you we only take on cases of those we believe are innocent."

"He didn't do it." She was begging now, and a few people turned back to their work. This was hard to watch. I found myself walking towards the two of them.

"I'm sorry, it's a no. Sandra will see you out." The tears spilled over then as she tried to frantically wipe them away.

"How do you know he didn't do it?" My voice was soft as I approached. Michael and Lucy both turned their gaze to me. I tried to ignore Michael's hard glare; I couldn't ignore her sad eyes.

"I spoke to him, I thought he was guilty, too, until then, but it was obvious from seeing him." She sniffed. I believed her, I believed every word she said. We had lots of people come in to plead their cases, but there was something different about this. I really felt like she was telling the truth. I could pick on a liar instantly and nothing about her told me she was lying.

"I've already said no," Michael continued, his eyes still glaring at me.

He was hinting at me to walk away, but my feet stayed firmly in place.

"I can take the case." The words flew out of my mouth, leaving no time for my mind to process them.

"Really?" Lucy's eyes widened as a hint of a smile crept onto her face. Relief flowed through her expression which made me smile despite my nerves.

"The Murray case," Michael reminded me, a warning in his tone.

"I can do both," I said confidently, although I didn't feel it inside. Michael sighed loudly.

"On your head be it." He wasn't happy with me, that much was obvious. I knew I was going to get my ass handed to me when Lucy wasn't between us. I was grateful she was now. *She needed me.*

"Thank you." Her voice was breathless as she reached for my hand with both of hers. "Thank you," she said again, softly squeezing my hand. As much as I wouldn't enjoy being yelled at, I knew I made the right decision. Lucy needed my help and I wanted to give it.

Beautiful women will be the death of me.

Eight

Lucy

Another sleepless night came my way as I couldn't stop my head from spinning. I wrote down everything I could think of that might help my father. Tomorrow was the day I would be knocking down doors in the hope someone would help me. There were five firms on that list, surely *one* of them would be able to take my father's case.

The next morning, I put on one of my favourite dresses, hoping it would improve my mood. Sadly, it didn't quite have the effect I was hoping for as I looked at myself in the mirror. I looked awful. I attempted to make my hair look nice and put some makeup on my face, but it didn't do anything to hide the exhaustion. I needed these people to listen to me, not pity me.

I had told my mother of my plans for the day and she hasn't spoken to me since. As sad as that made me, I am still just as determined, if not more, to prove my father's innocence. If she wouldn't go to bat for him, then I would. I was the only one he had left fighting for him now. It was a lonely existence.

The first two firms on the list wouldn't even see me. As soon as they heard my father's name, the receptionist quickly asked me to leave. My father's crimes had made it to the paper that morning, but I couldn't bring myself to read the articles. I didn't want to know what they said about him, what they said about us. He hadn't had his trial yet, but apparently *innocent until proven guilty* was lost on the majority. Our family would probably be shunned from the community. I had already made the decision not to even think about returning to college until I proved his innocence.

Part of me hoped that when I got home, I would hear some messages from my friends on my answering machine. Asking me if I was okay and offering their support. I knew that wasn't likely, no one would want to be associated with the daughter of a murderer.

I managed to get a meeting with both the third and fourth firm, but they took a similar turn. No matter what I said or put in front of them, they had written him off as guilty. None of them had the 'time' or 'resources' for cases that were likely to have a guilty verdict. He would only be a burden to them.

Despite the ache in my chest, I remained determined. I wasn't going to let them see me cry, I wanted them to see that I was strong. That I meant what I was saying. I may have been vulnerable in this moment, but I was not weak. My father was innocent and somebody was going to listen to me. Somebody *had* to listen to me.

I did my best to hold my head up high as I entered the last building. I could feel the tears threatening to build, but I took a deep breath.

Dad needs you to hold it together, Lucy.

Lucy

I did my best to ignore the stares as Michael Sawyer led me into a meeting room.

"Can I get you anything to drink?" I shook my head. "So, I imagine you are here to speak to me about your father?" he questioned.

"I am." I pulled the pieces of paper I had prepared out. "I wanted to talk to you about taking his case." He held his hand up to me.

"I won't take the case, Lucy." His voice was soft but the words still hit me heavily.

"You haven't let me talk yet." I felt desperation start to creep into my voice. *If he just listened to me.*

"I have another big case my firm needs to focus on, we cannot take any more on." He took a deep breath. "Truthfully, Lucy, I also think your father is guilty."

"He isn't, if you just let me explain—"

"I'm sorry, Lucy," he interrupted.

Frustration was beginning to overwhelm me. He wasn't listening to me, why wouldn't he listen to me? If he gave me five minutes, I could explain everything. He was my last hope.

"Please, we can prove his innocence. I need this." Desperation was seeping out of me, I felt pathetic. I was practically begging this man to listen to me. He stood up from his chair and headed to the door.

"I hope you have better luck elsewhere." I could feel the softness starting to leave his voice, he was becoming frustrated with me. That only made me more determined.

"This is the last place on my list," I continued. "I need your help." Without responding, he opened the door and started to walk out. The audience for our conversation suddenly got larger, but this didn't stop me. I continued to beg him to listen to me as we walked into the foyer. I was convinced I had lost when I heard a man's voice behind me.

"How do you know he didn't do it?" His voice was calm and I turned to face him. He looked at me with a soft expression. *He seemed kind.* There was something about him that made me unable to look away.

"I spoke to him, I thought he was guilty, too, until then, but it was obvious from seeing him," I said, trying to gather myself after I allowed the tears to spill. I was grateful that someone was listening to me, someone was asking me questions. Not just dismissing me without a second thought.

I nearly dropped to my knees when he said he would take on the case. *Someone believed me.* I could tell Michael wasn't happy with this man, but it didn't seem to stop him. He didn't miss a beat in taking this on. My last hope was standing in front of me and I allowed myself to smile just a little. There was still a long road ahead of me, but I at least had a start now.

He motioned me towards his desk away from Michael. If looks could kill, my last hope would be gone.

"I'm James Weatherston." He offered me his hand as he introduced himself.

"Lucy Davis," I said, accepting his hand.

"I know, I read about your father this morning." My breath hitched. He knew about my father's crimes already, but he was still willing to help me?

"Listen." His voice was quiet. "I can't talk about it now as I have to focus on another case today, but are you free tonight? Maybe we could get dinner and you could tell me more about your father?" He motioned to the papers in my hands.

"That would be great, thank you so much." I didn't know what words to say to express how grateful I was to him.

Lucy

"You don't need to thank me. Just go home and try to get some rest for now, we will start to help your dad later." He smiled softly and his kindness made me want to cry all over again.

"I will, than—" I stopped myself before I thanked him again. "Do you want to meet at the diner down the street at 7:00 p.m.?"

"Yes, *boss*," he said with a smirk. "I'll see you there. Take care of yourself, Lucy, okay?" I nodded. For the first time since I found out about my father, I felt hopeful. James was going to help me. *My last hope.*

Nine

James

I walked Lucy back out of the office before returning to face the wrath of Michael Sawyer.

"Weatherston, my office." His voice sliced through the room. All eyes were on me as I walked towards him. I felt like I was walking to my own death. I desperately wanted to escape the silent judging eyes of my colleagues.

"Sit," he said as I entered the room. I obliged and sat down quietly. "Have you been drinking today?" he questioned. I raised a confused brow at him.

"No, of course I haven't," I answered hesitantly, unsure where this was leading.

"I was just trying to find a reason for your stupidity just then." His voice raised. I sighed, feeling my heart pound. *Please don't fire me*, I thought to myself.

"Michael, I'm sorry. I just think there is a case there. What if he is innocent?" How could I not try? She clearly needed

James

us; how could he look her in the eyes and turn her away?

"Anthony Davis got himself a bit on the side and then killed her when the guilt started creeping in. It's an open and shut case, James. I've seen this hundreds of times."

"Something feels different about this." I knew nothing I was going to say would change his mind, but I felt I had to try. "I think she's telling the truth."

"She is telling *her* truth," he warned. "Of course, Daddy's little girl thinks he is innocent." I felt a rage start to build inside me at his words. I felt oddly protective over Lucy, despite just meeting, and I didn't like him speaking about her like that.

"I think she knows a lot more than you're giving her any credit for." He laughed which only enraged me more.

"Look, James, I like you and I think you have a lot of potential," he sighed. "You can take the case." I felt relief wash over me at his blessing. "But you do it on your own time, I don't want to see you working it during your work hours. When you're here, you're focused on Murray."

I nodded. Despite my anger towards his words about Lucy, I was grateful to still have my job. "Thank you."

I was disappointed that I had to work the case outside of my hours, as there weren't many hours as it was outside of here. I feel like I spend most of my life in this building. I had no idea how I was going to do it, but I had told Lucy I was going to help her. I was her last hope and I knew it.

The rest of my day was filled with filing—Michael's punishment for undermining him this morning. I was grateful to still have a job, so I did it without complaint. When I was finally done, I looked at my watch. 6:55 p.m.

Shit, Lucy.

I rushed out the door of the office heading down to the diner we agreed to meet at. Luckily, it wasn't too far and I was only a few minutes late. Lucy was already there, reading through the menu, seemingly lost in thought.

"I'm so sorry I'm late," I said breathlessly as I sat down.

"It's okay. I know you're probably really busy," she said lightly with a smile. She looked slightly less tired now, I hoped she managed to get some rest after the morning. Even though it had only been a few hours since I'd met her, I felt like I was just seeing her for the first time. The real her.

Not the her that was vulnerable and exhausted. Her eyes looked brighter. She hadn't touched up her makeup, but beauty still radiated from her. She was breathtaking to say the least.

She's your client, James, I reminded myself. Besides, her father was currently in prison being accused of murder. There were more important things in hand for both of us. This required my full attention.

"So can you tell me about your dad?" I asked after the waitress took our drinks order.

"Well, they said he drugged her and then—"

"Not about the murder," I interrupted. I already knew about it from the papers. "Tell me about *him*. About your childhood, favourite memories, everything. Helps me to build a picture of the kind of man he is," I said, offering her a small smile. I could tell she was nervous, I only hoped she didn't see how nervous *I* was. This was my first solo case and I was terrified. His future was in my hands and I felt the pressure of it on my shoulders. *How did Michael live like this all the time?*

I watched as she took a deep breath before starting again. I listened intently as she told me stories from her childhood. Tales of family holidays and happier times for their family.

James

The longer she went on, the wider her smile got. As if this reminiscing was helping her forget about the situation she was in. I would listen to her talk forever if it made her feel better. I couldn't even imagine the amount of pain she was carrying around in her heart, I wanted to help her fix it.

As she continued on telling a story about a fishing trip, a flash caught the corner of my eye. I turned to see a reporter taking the snap of us at the table. As I rose to my feet, he turned and ran.

"That's the second time that has happened today," Lucy said with a sigh. The joy on her face had been replaced with a sad expression once more. I clenched my fists as I sat back down.

"They are leeches, the whole lot of them." My voice came out harsher than intended.

"It's to be expected." She reached out and touched my hand. I realised how unprofessional I was being, letting my emotions show like this. My poker face really did need some work.

"I've been talking your ear off about my childhood, did you not want to talk about the case?" I brought my thoughts back to the moment.

"Not until after I've spoken to your father. They've moved him to jail now, but I've booked a meeting for tomorrow evening." Despite Michaels warnings, I had been doing some work on this case secretly. "When facing a jury, it is good to know as much about him from the people who love him, I know more about the person I'm defending and what they have at stake. Helps to build empathy."

"That makes sense. I probably went a bit overboard, didn't I?" she said with a laugh.

"No, Lucy, you were perfect. I got exactly what I needed." Her wide grin took over her face once more. I liked the fact my words put it there.

"Thank you, I know you told me not to thank you, but I'm grateful. You're the first person to even sit down and listen to me." I felt a twinge in my chest. A mixture of anger and pride fighting. Anger because nobody else was taking her seriously and pride because she trusted me. She trusted me to be the man who freed her father.

Ten

Lucy

I felt like a weight had been lifted off my chest as I took the bus back home. I nearly hadn't bothered going to the fifth firm after the previous rejections, but now I was glad I did. I only hoped I hadn't gotten James in too much trouble by taking on the case.

I walked back into the house to the sound of my mother moving around quickly upstairs.

Making my way into the bedroom, I saw her packing her things into a suitcase.

"Aunty Mel has said we can come and stay for a little while to get away from all of it," she stated in a matter-of-fact way. "I had a photographer snap my picture today as I was walking," she said with a sigh. "It's not going to be safe for us to stay here, so pack your things."

"I can't go with you," I said hesitantly. Aunty Mel's was a five-hour drive. Leaving town would mean I wouldn't be able to help James with the case. If I wasn't there, he would drop it. My father needed me. I understood my mother's need to get away, but we could stay close by. We didn't need to go that far.

"Why not?" Frustration was clear in her voice as she spoke.

"I found a lawyer today; he's going to take on Dad's case pro-bono and help prove he is innocent." With a loud crash, my mother knocked the suitcase onto the floor. Her face filled with anger like I'd never seen it before and I found myself instinctively taking a step backwards towards the door.

"When are you going to get it into your head that your father is guilty?" The volume of her voice made me jump. "He is a monster, Lucy; he doesn't deserve any help from you. Get on the phone and cancel that damn lawyer." There was venom in her tone, I had hoped she would be pleased. I knew she was angry with my dad. I was angry with him, too, regardless of his innocence in my mind. He was still having an affair. I wondered how much my mother knew before all of this. Was she aware that he had found someone else? That he *loved* someone else? She wrote him off quickly upon hearing the news. Part of me wonders if she was cheating on him, also. Were they both just putting on happy faces until I moved out? Has everything I've known about my parents been a complete lie?

I felt betrayed by both of them.

My parents had always represented the love I was striving to have one day. I wanted to be loved the way my father loved my mother. Now the thought makes me shudder. I was lost, completely and utterly lost. I don't think I've ever felt so alone in my entire life.

"I'm staying," I said firmly, matching her tone. "I'm staying.

Lucy

I'm meeting the lawyer tonight and I am going to help my father. If you want to run away from your problems then do it, but I will not see him rot. Not when I have a chance to make things right."

"I should have known you were your father's daughter." Out of context that would sound like a compliment, but in our situation it was a bitter insult. A knife to my chest. "You disappoint me, Lucy." And with those words, the knife twisted.

I didn't rise to her words as I made my way to my bedroom, slamming the door behind me. I laid on my bed and listened. It took a while, but eventually I heard the sound of her footsteps go down the stairs for the last time and out the door. She was gone, I was alone.

Just because a decision is hard, doesn't mean it's not the right one.

After a while, I decided to take James' advice and rest. There was nothing I could do in this moment and I needed to be rested if I stood a chance to help my dad. I needed to be at my best.

Luckily, I had the foresight to set my alarm next to my bed or I would have slept all evening. Rising out of bed, I realised I didn't have much time to get ready, just a quick freshen up. Given the state he saw me in earlier, I didn't think James would mind all that much.

When I went downstairs, I realised my mother had left Cato behind. I would say she did it to keep me company, but truthfully, she never really liked him. He was my father's dog, fundamentally.

Now it appears we were both abandoned by our family.

I walked out my front door and was greeted by a flash. The photographer took a few more pictures without saying a word.

I was too stunned to speak as I started heading towards the bus stop, quickening my pace as I did so. I turned my head; he was watching me, but didn't appear to be following me. I didn't like this feeling.

After getting the bus back into town, I had hoped James would be there already. Following the encounter outside my house, I didn't feel like being on my own. I didn't have to wait long before he rushed through the door with apologies.

At James' encouragement, we spoke for a while about my childhood with any stories I could remember. I felt comfortable talking to him.

When I looked at him, the same thought I had earlier popped back in. *He looks kind.* He was kind, he actually listened. Not just in the way some people do, but he was engaging with me, asking questions about what I was saying. He seemed genuinely interested in my words. *It felt like he cared.*

Midway through a story, there was another flash and my heart dropped. I tried to play it cool, but I was frightened. I was frightened to be on my own with reporters hanging around.

Lucy, you need to be brave. Your dad needs you.

James made it easier to be brave, it felt nice not to be completely alone in this situation. He was going to help me. It was strange how a man I met just a few hours ago now seemed like the only person I had left in the world.

"Where abouts are you parked? I'll walk you back in case that reporter is still out there," James said as he finished paying the check, despite my protests. I know I'm a college student, but I can't imagine his job paid him that well given they only did pro-bono cases.

"I took the bus. It's fine, I'll be okay walking on my own."

Lucy

His eyebrows raised in response.

"No, I'll drive you home. My car is just down the street."

"Oh, James, no. I live on the other side of the city, it's way too far," I protested.

"I'm taking you home, *boss,*" he said as he put his suit jacket back on. "You are not going home on your own with leeches like that reporter around. It's not safe." As I tried to argue, he put up his hands. "I'm insisting."

I gave up trying to fight, I had a feeling James Weatherston was just as stubborn as I was. It was going to be interesting working on my father's case together. As we got into his car, I decided it was his turn to tell me more.

"Have you always lived in the city?" I asked as he pulled away.

"No, I grew up in Rosehaven, just an hour outside of here." I'd heard of it, but I'd never been. "My folks still live there now."

"Do you have any siblings?" As an only child, I was always interested in other people's families. It was lonely being an only child, I hoped one day I would have a big family of my own. He hesitated before he answered.

"I have a sister, although she died a few years back." I suddenly felt awful for asking him the question.

"I am so sorry."

"It's okay, you didn't know." I could see a smile start to creep on his face, seemingly brought on by his memories. "I don't talk about her much, but I know I should. Her name was Alice. I might be biased, but she was a great big sister. She was always so determined, tenacious, I guess. I always looked up to her, wished I could be more like her."

He was quiet for a beat. "She died in a car crash; we were

both in the crash, but the drunk driver hit her side." My heart ached for him. Surviving something that took someone you loved away must be an awful feeling.

"Thank you for sharing that with me, I know it can't have been easy."

"Thank you for listening," he said, the sad smile still lingering on his face. The conversation continued and we moved onto lighter topics. He told me about Rosehaven and his best friend, Daines, who was back there. It was clear from how he spoke how fond he was of him. He seemed to miss his home. As we approached my house, I looked around, but I couldn't see any reporters.

"I'm going to pick you up tomorrow evening for you to come visit your father with me." He saw me about to speak and interrupted. "You are not taking the damn bus. You need to go anywhere, you call me." He reached into his pocket and pulled out his card. "Both my house phone and work phone are on there. If you need to talk about anything, you ring me."

"Thank you, I appreciate it," I relented. I wasn't going to fight and push away the only person looking out for me. We said our goodbyes and I headed inside the house. I noticed he didn't drive away until I was completely inside my home. It was sweet, really. The house was eerily quiet without either of my parents. I'm not sure how long I would be able to cope here alone. I decided to sleep on the sofa closer to the front door and the phone. *Just in case.* Cato curled himself up by my side. At least I wasn't completely alone here.

Eleven

James

Spending time with Lucy made me realise just how lonely I had been in this city. My life consisted of going to work and going through case files. Sure, I spoke to my colleagues, but that was always about work. We never discussed the ins and outs of our lives; I barely knew if any of them were married or what they liked to do in their off time. Truthfully, there wasn't much off time that came with this job.

Talking to Lucy tonight was the first time I'd had an in-person conversation about more than just work since before I can remember. I spoke to Daines on the phone often, but I hadn't sat down and spoke to someone in the longest time. It felt good.

It felt nice to talk about Alice, too. I didn't want her existence to be forgotten from this world. Daines always tried to probe me about her, but I shut him down quickly every time. I wouldn't do that again.

Despite the circumstances, I was grateful to have met Lucy Davis today and in a weird way, I was looking forward to seeing her tomorrow. To have more conversations not just about the case, but about her. I wanted to know *everything*.

When I got home, I had the urge to call Daines. I had no idea if he would be around, but I grabbed the phone off the wall and dialled anyway. His tired sounding voice answered the phone with a hello.

"Hey, Daines, sorry it's late. It's James."

"Hey, Weatherston, you okay? What happened?" His voice filled with concern. It wasn't like me to call this late; I didn't really think about that before dialling.

"I'm all good, sorry I just." My voice stuttered slightly. "I just had an urge to talk to you, I should have waited till morning. Sorry, I'll call you then."

"Don't you hang up on me." His voice was stern. "You're going to talk to me. What's on your mind?"

"I did something today that could potentially be the stupidest thing I've ever done."

"James Weatherston, doing something stupid? Well, I am shocked!" Daines said mockingly. "What did you do?"

"Have you heard about Anthony Davis?"

"It's all most people talked about at the station today."

"His daughter came in today, asking Michael to take the case. Michael refused to take it."

"Well, I'm not surprised by that. It sounds like a pretty clear-cut guilty charge, why would he take it?" I went silent as his words.

I heard him sigh. "You took the case, didn't you?"

"Yeah, I took the case."

"James," he groaned. "What were you thinking?"

James

"I believed her."

"Believed who?"

"His daughter, Lucy. I believed that she knew he was innocent. I sat and spoke to her tonight about everything. You would believe it, too, if you'd spoken to her. I know you would. After everything she told me, I think there is a chance he actually is innocent."

"Of course, she thinks he's innocent. He's her father. She's probably still in shock from finding out the news, it must be an awful feeling." I'd thought about that concept all day. How I would feel if I was in her shoes. If I woke up one day to find out my father had killed someone. I don't know if I would be fighting his innocence or wiping his entire existence from my brain.

"You weren't there, Daines." My voice came out harsher than I intended.

"No, I wasn't," he said calmly. "Look, James, I trust your judgement. You're one of the smartest guys I know. But you're also one of the kindest guys I know and people can take advantage of that kindness. Are you sure this Lucy isn't just playing on that? Her dad is a potential murderer, she could be some kind of sociopath."

"*She's not*," I replied sternly. I felt protective over her again, just like I had this morning with Michael and the reporter. I wanted to keep her safe and I wasn't going to listen to people bad mouth her. Especially when they hadn't even met her.

"Okay, don't bite my head off, Weatherston," Daines said defensively. "Look, I'm just worried about you. You're going to burn yourself out. Will you promise me you'll be careful with all this? If you look into it and it's not looking likely that he's innocent, will you drop it?"

"I will be careful; I promise I'll drop it if I need to." I wasn't sure if that was a promise I could keep, but I would try. I knew he had my best interests at heart.

"You should get some sleep, James, I know I need to." He laughed lightly. "Look, anytime you need me, you call me. *Anytime*. If I'm not home, I'll pick it up as soon as I get the message."

"The same goes for you. Take care of yourself, brother." As we said our goodbyes, I felt a weight off my chest. Even if he didn't agree with the actions I'd taken, he was still there, supporting me. My circle may be small, but the people in it provided me with everything I needed. They were precious to me.

My mind wandered back to Lucy as I put the phone back on the receiver. Making my way into the bedroom, I sat down on my bed, exhausted from the day. I wondered if she would be getting any sleep tonight, but I can't imagine she'd slept a night since her dad's arrest. Was she sitting on the edge of her bed, right now, pondering the next move?

I was nervous to speak with her father. People were right—of course she believed he was innocent. Seeing and speaking to him would be the real test. He was going to need to convince *me* he was innocent. I needed to look at him and believe it. If that didn't happen, this was going to be difficult.

Regardless, I wasn't sure I could give up on Lucy. I think even if I only saw guilt in his eyes, I would want to help her. I am worried I'm digging myself a hole that I wasn't going to be able to find my way out of. This case was putting both my professional and personal life at risk. The question was, is this a risk I am willing to take?

Twelve

Lucy

I woke up the next morning a bag of nerves. Today I was going to see my father again, I was going to have to see him at his most vulnerable once more. At least James would be with me. It felt slightly less daunting knowing he would be by my side, leading all the questions. Today was an opportunity for my father to prove his innocence. I knew James believed me, but I needed him to believe my father. I only hoped I was making the right decision by trusting my father.

I decided to check the answering machine for the first time since the arrest. I had noted the blinking red light, even heard it ring a few times, but I couldn't bring myself to touch it. Before Mom left, I had hoped she would clear it, but she was just as frightened by that red light as I was. Now she was gone and I had no choice but to be the one who listened.

It was clear from the first few messages that reporters had

found our number. All of them wanted the same thing: an exclusive interview from the family of a monster. *Alleged monster.* As I continued on through, I held onto the hope that one of them would be from my friends. My heart sank when the end of the message's tone played. Not a single one of them had called or left me a message. My father was in prison, my mother had left me behind, and not one of my friends cared enough to reach out to me to ask if I was okay. I sat down on the kitchen table and allowed the sobs buried inside me to surface. My whole body shook as I felt my heart shatter into a million pieces.

Hours passed in the day and I found myself torn between tears and anger. One minute I wanted to throw things across the room and the next minute I was breaking down on the couch, crying again. As it hit lunch time, I just about managed to scarf down a sandwich. Last night with James was the first proper meal I had eaten. I knew I needed to start to take better care of myself if I was going to help with the case.

After lunch, I decided I needed to pull myself together. I had done enough wallowing for one day. It was time to get myself ready for this evening. After a long shower, I started to write down notes to give to James. Detailing down first the stories I told him last night, I figured he was about to be overloaded with information. It would be easier if he had a written version to refer back to. I wanted to do whatever it took to help him free my father. This seemed to be the only thing I had left to focus on and I was going to give my all.

The time passed quickly and I jumped when I heard the doorbell go. When did it get this late? I checked myself quickly in the mirror, this was the best I'd looked in days to be fair. James was smiling at me as I opened the door.

Lucy

"Evening, boss. You ready?" He was wearing a smart suit and didn't look half as dishevelled as he did at dinner. Was it inappropriate to think your lawyer was attractive? I caught a whiff of cologne as I stepped out of the door.

"As I'll ever be," I said nervously. "Thank you for picking me up."

"Of course, it's about a twenty-minute drive to the jail," he said as we walked towards his car. "If you're lucky, I'll let you pick the radio station. Although if you pick jazz, you will be walking." I laughed in response as I climbed in the passenger seat.

"How about just one of the main stations?" I wasn't going to risk picking a bad choice and having to walk to the jail. James nodded and switched the radio on.

"I've written down everything I remembered about my dad from my childhood and some recent years' events," I said as we started driving. "I don't know if it's useful, but I just couldn't sit there all day and do nothing. I wanted to be useful."

He turned to smile at me briefly before focusing back on the road. "That is amazing, Lucy, thank you. It'll be a great help." I wasn't sure if he was saying that to make me feel better or if it was actually true. "Write down anything you think of and I can go through it. I'll take as much help as you are willing to give."

"Well, I quite literally have nothing else to do and my mother skipped town, so I am at your service."

"You're all alone in that house?" Concern filling his voice.

"She left yesterday afternoon, went to my aunt's house about five hours away. She isn't exactly overjoyed at the fact I am trying to prove Dad's innocence; I think hiring a lawyer was the final straw." I tried to be light hearted in tone, but I could feel my sadness seeping through.

"Lucy, I am so sorry. Why didn't you say something yesterday? I don't want to cause you or your family any more stress."

"It's not your fault, James," I said, shaking my head. "I think there are many things about my parents and their marriage that I didn't know about, *don't* know about. I think my mother was looking for a way out and this was it," I sighed. "Besides, it isn't your fault. You're the only one who is helping me." I gave a weak laugh. "Also, I am not completely alone, Cato is there."

"Cato?" he questioned.

"Our dog, well, he was Dad's dog. He seems to be the only one who hasn't abandoned me."

He was quiet for a moment and I was worried I was making him regret his decision to help me.

"I'm not going anywhere, Lucy; we are going to see this thing through *together*." He paused. "No matter what the outcome." I could tell he was hesitant in his last sentence. I knew there was every chance we wouldn't be able to prove my father's innocence. I also knew there was still a chance he was guilty.

"You don't have to; I would understand if you wanted to back out. This isn't your mess to clean up."

"It's not yours, either, yet here you are." He was nervous, his fingers tapping the steering wheel. " It takes a special kind of person to fight for someone like this. To be willing to go to bat for them when no one else will."

"It takes a special kind of person to take on a case, even though I know it got him in trouble with his boss," I countered. I saw a smile across his face.

"Well, since we both now have elevated egos, should we go

see what your father has to say for himself?" I looked out the window and saw we were closing in on the jail.

"Let's get to work, Weatherston."

Thirteen

James

I tried my best to keep my nerves from showing on my face as we were escorted into a room to wait for Anthony. I pulled the chair back for Lucy to sit before sitting myself. Placing my notepad on the table, I began to doodle. I always liked to draw pictures when I needed the distraction. I caught Lucy peering over my shoulder.

"That's really cute," she said, pointing to the dog I was drawing on the page. "Can you draw people, too?" I gave a shrug.

"I can, but I don't really draw properly. I just like to doodle on a page."

"Maybe you can draw me someday," she said teasingly. Before I could respond, the door opened and I watched as a large man in an orange jumpsuit entered. It was a fair assumption this was Lucy's father.

"Who is this?" His eyes darted between me and his daughter.

James

"This is James, he's the lawyer who is going to be taking on your case."

I tried to read his face, a sense of relief and anxiety battling each other for the prime spot on his expression.

Anxiety seemed to be winning. Everyone was silent for a beat; I'd never been in this position before. If I was honest, I wasn't really sure what I was supposed to do.

"Sorry, I was just expecting someone older." Anthony broke the silence with words that made the atmosphere even more tense than it already was. He doubted my ability, which was fair, because I was also starting to doubt myself. I was completely out of my depth here. I'd only just graduated, for fuck's sake. *What was I doing here?*

"James works for Michael Sawyer's firm; he was one of the pro-bono firms from the leaflet," Lucy said, clearly attempting to ease the tension.

"Isn't he the same lawyer working on the Murray case?" I gave a quick nod. "I saw that on the news before I..." He paused. *Before he was arrested.* "Does Michael have the time for both cases? He must be a busy man."

"Actually, it's me personally who has taken on the case," I hesitated. "Outside of my work at Sawyer's." Anxiety was definitely winning the battle on his face. He didn't trust me and well, I didn't trust him, either.

As I sized him up, there was something about him that made me feel uneasy. I couldn't place it. He was a large man, killing Amber would have been light work for him. He was softly spoken, I'll give him that, but I was hoping I'd be immediately convinced of his innocence. *I wasn't.*

"I'd like to ask you some questions about the night of Amber's murder." I paused to read his face. I wanted to see how he looked when I said her name. He seemed genuinely sad, almost like he was longing for her. "You saw her that night, right? Tell me about it."

His gaze shifted between Lucy and I. Should I have brought Lucy with me? My gaze fell to her next to me, she was staring straight ahead at her father. There may be things he wasn't willing to say in front of her.

"I went around her house and we had dinner together before I went home." His eyes were now on the table. I knew this wasn't the first Lucy was hearing about his affair, but it can't be an easy thing to hear. I resisted the urge to place my hand on hers.

"Did you drink together that night?"

"We had some red wine with dinner, but only a glass or two." Amber was found to be drugged with some kind of sleeping pill, likely given to her through her drink. Amber had not been prescribed any pills, but I knew Lucy's father had. I had only had a brief overlook of the files released by the police, but I knew both of Lucy's parents had been prescribed sleeping pills. I'd like to think a killer would be smarter than to use their own supply, but it wouldn't be the first time someone had made a mistake like this.

"Was there a reason you didn't stay longer? Is it normal for you to leave at that time?" According to his police statement, he left at 10:00 p.m., but Lucy's mother, Vera, shared in her statement that she didn't notice him come in until after midnight. Amber Jones only lived twenty minutes from Lucy's house.

"I had told Vera I was only working until ten, so it would have looked suspicious if I had come home too late. Sometimes I stay later, it depends on what time I am expected home."

James

My eyes briefly looked at Lucy and I could see hers brimming with tears as her father spoke. All this time they thought he was at work when in reality he was living another life without them.

"Vera said you were home after midnight. What did you do between leaving Amber's and going home?" I questioned.

"I got home at ten-thirty, not after midnight. I came straight home from Amber's." I could see him gritting his teeth as he spoke.

"That is not what Vera said. She said you were home after midnight," I repeated.

"Vera is mistaken." His voice was harsh back to me.

"Why would she say you were home after midnight if you weren't?" I knew I was angering him, but I continued my line of questioning. I wanted to see his temper, the man underneath. I wanted him to show me who he really was. If the monster was inside of him, I was going to let it out of its cage.

"I don't know, she wasn't even…" He cut himself off. "She was mistaken." *She wasn't even what?* I wondered. I tried to ignore Lucy's presence now as I continued, she wasn't going to like this.

"How many other women other than your wife were you sleeping with, Anthony?" I felt both their eyes on me. There was something about Anthony that wasn't quite right, I wanted him to show me his teeth. I was willing to throw my professionalism out the window. If he wasn't willing to bare all to me, I wouldn't be able to help him. *I wouldn't be able to help Lucy.*

"There was only Amber at the time, no one else," he spat. "I had seen other women previously, but not recently."

"Well, no one else but your wife at home," I reminded him. His fist slammed on the table which gained him being told off from the guard behind him. A reminder to calm down or he would be taken away. A reminder to him that he was not in control here. *I was.*

"I loved Amber," he said after collecting himself. "I was going to leave Vera for her and start afresh," he finished, looking back down at the table. As I eyed Lucy next to me, I spied her leg bouncing up and down awkwardly. I could see how tense she was just from a quick glance. I wanted to continue to push Anthony, but I was not going to upset Lucy further. She deserved better than to witness this. I would come back without her tomorrow.

"I think I have everything I need for now."

"That's it? You have hardly asked me anything useful!" His voice raised. "Lucy, where did you find this idiot?" His distaste for me was evident from the moment I walked in. I didn't care if he liked me or not. I wasn't doing anything of this for him, I was doing it for Lucy.

Lucy sat quietly; I had half hoped she may come to my defence, but as I looked at her watery eyes, I could tell she wasn't even here. Her mind was no longer in this room. I couldn't even imagine all the things that she was thinking about right now. I needed to get her out of here, this wasn't doing her any good.

"I will be seeing you soon, Anthony. I look forward to working with you." My words dripped with sarcasm as I got out of my chair. Lucy still didn't move, so I lightly tapped her on the arm. She jumped at my touch, but quickly came back to her senses. I held her arm as I helped her out of the chair, not letting go of it as we walked out to the car. She didn't even acknowledge her father as we left.

Fourteen

Lucy

Most girls my age right now were nervous to bring their boyfriends home to meet their fathers. In my world, I was nervous to bring a lawyer who I was becoming friends with to meet my father in prison. This isn't quite how I envisioned my life turning out.

I tried to keep quiet as much as possible when they spoke, even in the moments where I was angry. My own father betrayed our family. He was going to leave Mom. *Leave us.* The only thing he seemed to regret was the fact he left Amber's house that night, not the damage he has done. I was grateful to be back out in the fresh air and I purposely walked slowly back to James' car.

It was becoming glaringly obvious that even if we proved his innocence, my life would never be the same again. My father's actions outside of Amber's murder changed everything.

"Are you okay, boss? That was heavy stuff back there." James

Lucy

broke the silence; his voice was so calming to me. I nodded, but I couldn't find any words. I felt like I was completely talked out about my father and this situation. I wanted a break from it. I found myself zoning out when they were talking. Hearing my father's plans to leave us shattered me. I didn't know how to process these emotions; I was just grateful I wasn't alone right now.

"Are you hungry?" My silence didn't deter him from continuing. "We can stop for something to eat on the way back?" James was sweet, part of me wished we had met under different circumstances.

"That sounds great, I'm sorry he was a bit tough on you in there." I could tell from almost the moment we walked in my father did not like James. He didn't trust that he was capable of getting him off the charges.

Truthfully, when I first met James, I had my doubts in his ability. He was barely older than me and seemed nervous at every step. But it was his courage that won me over. The courage to stand up to his boss and take the case even though he knew it would get him in trouble. He took the case despite his lack of experience. He sat in front of my father, who was an intimidating man, and did his best to help him. He sat there and held his own against him, even if his line of questioning took me by surprise.

If I were to do it again, I would take a man like James over any of those other lawyers I saw, especially Michael.

I would take a man who was brave over a man who was overconfident .

"Nothing I can't handle," he said shyly, a slight red tint on his cheeks. I paused when we got to his car. "Are you okay?" He noticed my hesitation. He seemed to be in tune to my feelings.

"No. I don't know if I will ever be okay again." I let out a breath as I leant against his car. I felt him come close to me, his hand landing on the car right next to me. Leaning in closer to me, he spoke.

"I don't think you quite realise how strong you are, Lucy." He was so close I could feel the heat of his breath on my face. "I have honestly never met anyone who is as brave as you are, who could handle a situation like this the way you have. I know you must be hurting a lot inside, but you should be proud of yourself."

"I'm fine, really," I lied. My inside was constantly at war with itself, every single movement I took hurt.

I felt like I couldn't gather a single thought without my entire head exploding.

"You don't ever have to hide your pain from me, Lucy," he said, a hint of sadness in his voice. I knew he could tell I was lying. "I don't want you to just think of me as your dad's lawyer." My heart skipped a beat as I waited for him to continue. "I want you to think of me as your friend, too."

"I could really use a friend right now," I admitted. I was completely and utterly alone in the world, or at least I had been. Now I had James.

"Me too." He smiled. "I am here for you every step of the way, boss." We stayed with our eyes locked for a moment. I didn't want to pull away and he didn't seem to, either.

"I don't know about you, but I am starving," he said, finally moving away from me and opening the passenger door. I nodded and stepped into the passenger seat.

I had always believed that people fell into your life exactly when you need them. It was fate that James and I met earlier this week, I know it was.

Lucy

* * *

I was starting to run low on food, so the next day I made a run for the grocery store. Since my mother was gone with our only car, I had to take the bus there. I know James said to call him if I needed a ride anywhere, but I wasn't going to call him for something so trivial. I was fine on the bus.

I was convinced everyone was staring at me, that they all knew who I was and who I was related to. It was highly unlikely the random people on the bus knew my face. So far, the pictures that had been taken of me hadn't appeared in any of the papers. It was only a matter of time, however. I was more concerned about running into people I knew, I still had heard nothing from any of my friends.

I wondered if we managed to clear my father's name, would they magically pop back into my life? I don't know if I would want them back in it, honestly. No matter what my father has been accused of, I have done nothing. They abandoned me at a time when I needed them the most.

Besides, I didn't need them anymore. James and I were friends. I knew if I called him up, he would answer; he wouldn't dodge my calls. I knew he would stand there and listen to me all night if I needed him to.

My thoughts began to linger on James. I almost missed him; we had no plans to see each other today and my day felt empty without him. I guess I had just gotten used to having him around. I wondered if he had thought of me at all today. Would it be needy to ring him later? *Yes, Lucy, of course it would.* He was just being kind; he didn't actually want me on the other end of the phone 24/7. I couldn't believe how pathetic I was being. How did I get here?

The actual grocery store trip went off without a hitch. Despite my anxiety, nobody ran up to me and yelled about my father. People just went about their days as if everything was completely normal. It was nice to do something so mundane for a while.

As I got off the bus, I couldn't help but feel a pair of eyes on me. I started to walk towards my house and as I looked behind me, I could see two men in the distance. They were not being subtle about the way they stared at me with their arms folded. *Did they know who I was?* I started to walk quicker, as I did so, I noticed them started to move also.

Fuck.

There was absolutely no mistaking they were after me. I picked up my pace, sprinting now. I didn't dare look behind me to see if they had started to run, too. I fumbled, looking for my keys in my bag and bursting through the door, immediately locking it behind me.

Running to the backdoor, I checked everything was shut and locked before grabbing Cato and hiding out of sight of the window.

We sat crouched there as the minutes went by. I was waiting for someone to knock down the door, to come in and hurt me. I was only met with silence. Whoever they were, they were gone.

I hope.

Fifteen

James

As I sat in the office, I couldn't get my mind off of Lucy. We had talked in the car, eating our food for hours after leaving the prison. We kept the conversation away from her father, talking instead about our hopes and dreams. What we were looking forward to on the other side of this. I hoped I made her feel better, I wanted her to look to the brighter days. They were coming. We would work this out together and then she could move on with her life. She could go back to college or maybe transfer elsewhere to finish up her business qualifications. She would be okay once this was all over, I just knew it.

It was strange, the way I felt when I looked at her. Lucy made me feel hopeful, she had this calming and bright nature about her. When I was around her, everything just felt better. I'd never known anyone to make me feel like this before. I was a little lost without her right now, I wished we were together working on the case or even just talking. Instead, I was sitting here in an office with people I honestly don't think cared if I existed or not. I think I could disappear tomorrow and they wouldn't even notice. *Lucy would notice.*

My gaze fell to the phone on my desk. *Maybe I should call her.* Just to check in and make sure she was doing okay after yesterday. Last night was intense and I knew she was hurting, I wanted to help her. Selfishly, I also wanted to hear her voice, her laugh would make my day better. My hand hovered over the phone, but I thought better of it.

She had better things to do than talk to me. God, when did I get so pathetic? It had only been two days and I'm sitting here, pining over her. She was a client; I was doing my job. I knew better than to cross those lines, but seeing her last night, how upset she was about her father. She needed a friend and I wanted to be there for her. I knew I was blurring my responsibilities and Michael would lose his mind if he found out, but this was my choice. Being everything Lucy needed was my choice.

I was anxious to see her father tonight. I should have been working on the Murray case, but the Anthony Davis case consumed me. I did notice that he seemed sadder than I anticipated at her death. Things were usually so clear cut for me, but with him I still have questions.

When I sat in front of him, I found myself confused. On the one hand, there was nothing about him that led me to believe he was lying. He had a temper, sure, but the motive for killing Amber didn't seem to be there. He was about to start a new life with Amber, it wouldn't make sense for him to hurt her.

Despite this, he made me feel uneasy, like there was more than met the eye. I didn't feel comfortable around him, even with his own daughter in the room. Whatever I felt, I don't think Lucy felt it. Even with her anger, I don't think she noticed that something wasn't right about him.

I was determined to push him further today. I wanted the lion to show me his teeth. If I was going to defend him, I needed to know what I was up against. I needed to make sure Lucy didn't keep her expectations too high. I couldn't watch the inevitable heartbreak that would follow.

Work was over before I really got my head into anything and before I knew it, I was at the prison. My eyes wandered around the room whilst I waited for Anthony. I remember reading about how they often make rooms dark and cold on purpose. It helps to break down the suspect, get them to confess quicker. They would be so desperate to get out of the room they would say whatever they needed to.

"James." Anthony's voice broke my thoughts as he was dragged into the room. He looked even rougher than he did yesterday. The dark circles under his eyes mixed with bruising on his face. My eyes wandered down to his orange jumpsuit. *Not his colour,* I thought to myself.

"Anthony, good to see you." Let's hope he wasn't as good at telling a lie as I was. That was a bare faced one.

"Where is Lucy?" he questioned, looking at the empty seat next to me.

"I thought it was better that you and I talked alone."

"Very well." He let out a sigh as he sat down. "What would you like to know?"

"You loved Amber?" I asked, clearing my throat.

"With everything I had." His words made my chest twinge. I imagined how it would have felt for Lucy if she had heard that. Suddenly, I'm more affirmed in her lack of presence for today's meeting.

"You only were dating for a couple weeks before she died? How could you have been in love with her?"

"Have you ever been in love, James?" I shook my head. Truthfully, I'd barely been in relationships. A girlfriend here and there, but I'd always preferred the casual approach.

"If you had ever been in love, you would understand. One minute you feel like you are dragging yourself through life, and the next, they walk into it and everything changes. All those things you thought mattered, don't. The only thing that matters is them and you would do anything for them."

His words left a bitter taste in my mouth. He could paint it any way he wanted, but there was nothing romantic about what he said. Not when I knew one of those things that mattered before was Lucy. *His own daughter.* By his own admission, she was no longer important to him after he found Amber and it made me furious. He was going to leave her behind, even if Amber had lived. He still would have broken Lucy and her mother's hearts.

How fucking dare he sit here and lecture me. Maybe he wasn't a monster, or even a killer, but he still was a fucking asshole.

"How did it feel doing everything you did?" I asked, ignoring his previous statement.

"How did it feel doing what, exactly?" he said impatiently.

"Fucking Amber and then going back home to face your wife and child? Did you hop straight into bed with Vera?" I noticed his fists clenched at my words.

"I am not proud of it. It didn't feel good," he said through gritted teeth.

"That didn't stop you from keeping on doing it, did you? To keep on betraying your wedding vows, time after time.

James

Betraying the people you claim to love." I was crossing the line and I knew it. He didn't deserve his family and I wanted him to go to bed tonight feeling guilty for everyone he had hurt.

His fists slammed on the table "Enough!"

"Were you still sleeping with your wife after you met Amber? Or did you decide you didn't love her as soon as something prettier came along?"

"What the fuck does this have to do with my case?" Frustration seeping into his words. "Fuck you!" He launched himself across the table, but the guard was quicker, pulling him back down. There it was. I was in the lion's den and he was *finally* showing me his teeth. I had him exactly where I wanted him.

He was silent for a few beats as he calmed down. "I didn't kill Amber," he whispered with a sigh.

"I know," I replied smugly, his eyes staring into mine.

"If you know, why are you asking me all these stupid questions?"

"Because unless we figure out who really killed Amber, you will be going to trial. You will have to stand in front of a jury, facing cross examination a lot worse than what I just did. If you stand a hope in hell of proving your innocence, you cannot lose your cool like that. Do you understand me?" I scolded.

"I understand," he said like a child who had just been told off by a teacher. I think the reality is only just starting to kick in. This wouldn't be over any time soon. Without finding out who really killed Amber, we were going to trial. We would spend days, if not weeks in that courtroom. It was going to be exhausting for everyone involved. If he behaved like that, there was no hope for him. He would immediately be seen as aggressive.

"Did Vera know about Amber?" Vera was my other worry. Legally, wives did not have to testify against their husbands, but their relationship was not good. The prosecution would have a field day if she agreed to testify.

"No." He shook his head. "I think she knew there was sneaking around, but not specifics. To be honest, I was suspicious she was sneaking around, too."

Poor Lucy, was the first thought that came to my head. If we went to court finding evidence that Vera was *also* having an affair, it would be crucial. It would help the jury feel less sympathy for her.

"Your daughter seems to be the only good thing that came out of you and Vera." I struggled to hide the bitterness in my voice. I had already crossed the line of professionalism, there was no going back now. I got to my feet, I was over this conversation.

"Just make sure you control your temper in future," I added as I started to walk out.

"I don't think I am the only one with a temper, James," he shot back.

"Well then you best hope you stay on my good side."

Sixteen

Lucy

I felt completely cooped up in my house, especially alone. It was starting to feel like *I was the one* alone in a prison cell. My father may be the one trapped physically, but being trapped in my own head was crushing me. I was trying to claw out of my own brain, but I couldn't escape.

I decided to go for a walk, I would do anything to free myself from these suffocating walls. It had been a few days since I had taken Cato out and we both needed the fresh air. It was just after dinner and I hoped the neighbourhood would be quiet. Most people walked earlier in the day; I had watched them all passing by my window. I was alone, just watching the world go by.

Earlier in the day, I had listened to the messages, nothing but reporters. Not even my own mother had called to check up on me.

"You have my full permission to bite anyone with a camera,"

I said to Cato as we exited the door. A few days ago, I loved going out for walks with Cato, walking down to the fields by our house. Getting some fresh air after a long day of college. Now every step away from my front door increased my anxiety. I was frightened to leave my own house. What had happened to me?

Even though I wasn't the one behind bars, I felt like I was being punished. I passed only a handful of people on my way to the fields, but each one made me feel jumpy. I was poised, ready to defend myself in case they whipped their camera out, or worse, in case they shouted at me.

My neighbour a few doors down was taking his trash out, he stared hard at me as I walked past.

"Scum," were the words that left his mouth as I passed. I ignored him and fought the urge to turn around and run home. None of this was my fault, but all of the consequences seemed to fall on me. Maybe I should have run away with my mother.

I let Cato off his lead as we entered the field. I enjoyed the sight of him running around. He looked free, he looked happy. I wish I could feel like he did right now. That feeling of freedom with no worries. I felt bad for the fact I had kept him cooped up with me, it wasn't fair for him.

I was so distracted watching Cato that I didn't hear the person behind me approach. Before I knew it, I felt hands on my shoulders, forcing me towards the floor. I let out a scream, but a hand quickly covered my mouth.

"Do you know what your father did?" a male voice yelled at me. He had tried to hide his face with a mask, but I could see his eyes clearly. His hands moved to my throat and I struggled for air. Panic was flowing through me, I tried to thrash, but I couldn't move. He had his entire weight pressed into me.

Lucy

"This is how Amber felt when he killed her," he spat at me. "Now he's going to know how it feels to lose *everything*." I wanted to scream, to cry out, but I couldn't. I was going to die and the last thing I was going to see were his eyes.

This was how Amber died.

Just as I had given up thrashing, I heard Cato barking. My eyes caught sight of him as he jumped towards the man, biting down on his leg.

"Fuck!" he said, falling off of me, his hands moving away from my neck. *I was free*. As I struggled for breath, I scrambled onto my feet. Adrenaline was pumping through me as I started to run back towards my house, Cato at my heels. I didn't stop until I made it back through my door, slamming it shut. I locked it and collapsed in front of it. The weight of what just happened dawned on me.

He tried to kill me because of what he thought my father had done. *I was in danger.*

Sobs found their way out of me as I pulled my knees to my chest, rocking myself back and forth to calm myself down. Cato stayed close to me, attempting to lick my face for comfort. It made me laugh slightly. When I had calmed down, I found my way to the window, checking to see if the man was there. The street was quiet, but I still felt terrified.

I needed help. *I needed James.*

I found his number on the card he'd given me and dialled. He answered and even the sound of his hello made me feel safer.

"James, it's Lucy." There was a slight crack in my voice as I spoke.

"Lucy?" His concern was evident in his voice. "Are you okay?"

"No..." I said swallowing hard, biting back my tears. "I'm sorry, I didn't know who else to call."

"You have nothing to be sorry for, I told you could call me anytime about anything." His voice was soft and I knew I had made the right choice in calling him. "Tell me everything, sweetheart."

So, I did. I couldn't hold it together as I retold the story of what had happened to me. I kept having to pause to wipe away my tears and James would tell me to take my time. He listened to every word I was saying and didn't make me feel rushed.

"Lucy," he said with a shake in his voice when I finally finished.

"Yes?"

"Pack a bag, I'm coming to get you."

Seventeen

James

I felt like my heart was in my throat as soon as Lucy told me about being followed and what happened. Rage filled every inch of me and I wanted to find him. I wanted to make him pay for thinking he could hurt her like that. *He deserved to be punished.* I would not have previously described myself as a violent man, but if I had been there, I would have made him hurt for going near her. For even laying a single finger on her head.

I needed to get to her, I needed to keep her safe. When I thought of a safe place to go, my first thought was Rosehaven. It was the safest town I knew. My parents had a cabin by the lake; it was a little run down, but no reporters would be able to get to us there. *Lucy would be safe there with me.*

I thought about taking her back to my place, but aside from the fact I was embarrassed of my apartment, it also wasn't far enough away from the danger of the city and its people. I needed to get Lucy away from the city completely.

I also wasn't going to subject Lucy to staying with my parents, we would not get any work done with them lingering. Besides, I wasn't in the headspace to deal with them pressuring me about work.

I debated calling my father for permission to use the cabin, but decided against it.

Easier to ask for forgiveness than permission. We would eventually go see them once we were settled.

I'd like to think he would want to see me; I honestly can't remember the last time I saw them.

Daines had been asking me to come back home, also. Maybe he could help out with the case a little; it would be interesting to get his perspective.

I couldn't think too much about that now, I needed to get to Lucy. I rushed into my room, throwing an assortment of clothes in a bag. Worse case, I could come back here if I needed to. The most important thing right now was getting Lucy away.

When I finished packing, I raced down to my car. It was only as I was driving over that I thought about work.

Shit, Michael was going to kill me.

No, it would be fine. I'd call him tomorrow from the cabin and explain why I had to go back home. He would understand, I am sure he would. He couldn't be that much of an asshole that he wouldn't see I had no choice here. I pushed the thoughts of work out of my mind. There was nothing I could do about it now, it was tomorrow's problem.

I pulled up outside and immediately headed to the front door.

"Lucy, it's me," I said as I knocked. I wouldn't be surprised if she ignored me if I didn't announce myself. She must be feeling so frightened.

"James," she said breathlessly as she opened the door. It was obvious she had been crying. I could see the marks around her neck and rage filled me all over again. Instinctively, I wrapped my arms around her and pulled her close into me. She accepted the embrace and began to cry softly into my chest.

"James, I was so scared," she said in between sobs.

"It's okay. I'm here now, you're safe with me. I won't let anyone hurt you, I promise." I squeezed her tighter, wanting to hold her until she felt better. Until she believed me that she was safe. Lucy would always be safe as long as I was around.

She insisted she didn't want to call the police; she didn't want to draw any more attention to herself. I protested, but ultimately gave in. She was with me now, that was what mattered.

"Why did you tell me to pack a bag?" she asked, composing herself.

"We are going to go to Rosehaven for a few days, we'll finish working the case there and get you away." I wasn't mentioning it as if it was a choice, because it wasn't. I was getting Lucy out of here, no matter what.

"Under different circumstances, I'd call that a lovely vacation." She laughed lightly, prompting a small laugh from me.

"Have you got everything ready?" She moved towards her bag, picking it up to show me with Cato following close behind her. I would be cooking that dog a steak dinner in Rosehaven, given he just saved her life. "Then let's get you out of here, boss," I said, reaching to take the bag from her hand. As we approached the car, I first opened the passenger door for her to get in before putting the bag in the trunk next to mine. I let Cato into the back seats.

I could tell she was still frightened and it made me want to reach for her, to hold her close. I would do anything to make Lucy Davis feel happy again.

We drove in silence for a while. It was late and emotions were running high after Lucy's experience.

"I don't know what I would have done without you," she said quietly. I gave in to my instincts and placed my hand on hers; she twisted hers round and squeezed mine. "I didn't even think of calling my mom, isn't that insane?" she sighed. "I just had the scariest experience of my life and it didn't even cross my mind to call my own mother."

She just had the scariest experience of her life and she chose to call *me*. I felt sad and honoured all at the same time.

"I'm glad you trusted me enough to call me."

"Do you want the truth?" she asked, making me feel nervous. "You seem to be the only person in the world I can trust right now."

My heart leapt as I couldn't help but gain a small smile. *Lucy trusted me.* I pulled her hand to my mouth, planting a small kiss.

"Why don't you close your eyes for a bit? I'll wake you up when we get there." I saw her nod in the mirror before resting her head back and closing her eyes.

As we arrived at the cabin, instinctively I grabbed her hand again after we were out of the car. Before I could pull it away, I felt her squeeze my hand.

"Give me the grand tour then, Weatherston." Her face beamed up at me as I turned to look at her. She was beautiful, truly and completely beautiful. I felt like the luckiest guy in

James

the world to even breathe the same air as her.

Eighteen

Lucy

I immediately felt a weight off my chest the second James knocked on the door. Everything was going to be okay.

I didn't hesitate to go with him—he didn't need to convince me that my house was not safe anymore. I was desperate to get out of there and I knew James would take care of me.

I held onto his hand as we walked into the cabin. It was a little run down, but even in the dead of night it was beautiful. I felt completely at peace here, there was nothing else around. Walking inside, I let go of his hand to explore, feeling a slight emptiness without it.

"Sorry it's not much..." James said shyly.

"It's perfect, James." I smiled at him, taking in the room. It was a small place, but it was exactly what I needed.

No one would be able to find me out here, whoever that man was wouldn't get near me again. We could work on the

Lucy

case in the safety of this cabin.

"I'll find some bedding for you; the bedroom is just through there if you want to drop off your stuff." I nodded and headed towards it, Cato following close behind. He wasn't usually a clingy dog, but in the last few days and especially since the attack, he was not leaving my side. I wasn't complaining.

"Wait, James, there's only one bedroom?" I questioned. The only other doors I could see led to the bathroom. The living room and kitchen were combined in the same area.

"Yeah, I'll crash on the couch. You and Cato can have the bedroom."

"James, I am not kicking you onto the couch in your own family's house. I can sleep there."

"It's cute you think this is up for debate, boss," he said as he entered the bedroom, bedding in hand. "You are sleeping in here and that is final. I will not let a lady sleep on a couch." He started to sort the bedding out for me. It was quite sweet watching him be domesticated. I didn't realise I was quite intently staring at him until he spoke again.

"Is there anything else I can get for you?" I shook my head as Cato jumped into the bed. He was clearly quite happy James was going to be the one on the couch.

"Sleep well, Lucy," he said as he started to walk about the door. "I'm just out here if you need anything, okay?"

"Thank you." I returned his smile as he closed the door. After getting changed, I climbed into bed next to Cato who was already fast asleep. It took a while, but eventually my mind was clear enough to drift apart. Knowing James was in the next room helped.

* * *

Till Death Parts Us

I couldn't breathe. It was there again, those hands pressing into my neck. All I could do was gasp as I felt myself go weak. I managed to open my eyes and the man was there again. His entire body weight on top of me as those eyes bore into me. They were dark and clouded over. This time he didn't speak, he just held his hands on my throat, pushing them as hard as he could. My eyes briefly flicked around the room, hoping Cato was still in here with me, but he was nowhere to be found.

I was going to die.

Tears streamed down my face as I lay there helpless. There was nothing I could do but let myself go.

I thought about Amber, what it was like for her in her final moments. Whoever killed her had her exactly like this, but to make it worse, it was in her own home. A place where she was supposed to feel safe. Images of her body that Detective Mason showed me flashed through my mind. Aside from the bruising on her neck, she didn't have any other visible injuries, meaning she didn't put up much of a fight. She must have known her killer; it didn't take her by surprise that they were there.

I would die before I ever found out what actually happened to her, before I helped my father be free.

"Lucy." A voice broke my thoughts, it sounded so close, but it wasn't the man with his hands on my throat. "Lucy!" There was more urgency in the voice now, but it was too late.

I could feel someone shaking me, willing me to open my eyes again. As I did, James was right next to me, one of his hands reached round my back as he brought the other one to my face. "Lucy," he said breathlessly, relief flooding his face.

"What happened?" I asked.

"You were screaming and I…" His voice was panicked as he

Lucy

spoke. He took a deep breath before continuing. "You must have been having a nightmare, but I thought someone was hurting you and then I couldn't wake you up." I watched as tears formed in his eyes as he cleared his throat.

"None of it was real," I said softly. The man from earlier hadn't come back. He hadn't found us here. I was only reliving the events of earlier.

"None of it was real," he repeated, brushing his hand through my hair as he pulled me tighter into him. I moved my head into his chest and let the sobs break free. With each sob, I felt him hold me even tighter. "It's okay, you're safe. It was just a dream. Everything is going to be okay," he whispered against my head.

"That man," I said, attempting to regain some composure. "He was here in the room; he was trying to kill me again," I said, gulping hard.

"He can't get you here, he can't get you when you're with me." There was a slight sternness in his voice, a determination to get me to believe him. He lifted up my chin so my eyes were locked with his. "Nobody can hurt you when you're with me. *Nobody*."

I did believe him; I believed every word. I believed he would do whatever it took to keep me safe. Nobody had ever made me feel like this before.

"James?"

"Yes, boss?" His nickname for me made me laugh softly.

"Will you stay in here with me tonight? I don't think I can be here alone."

"Of course." He briefly let go of me to get himself comfortable under the blankets before resuming his position holding me. "You're not alone, Lucy." His voice made me feel warm as I snuggled into his touch. This time around, I fell asleep quickly in the safety of his arms.

Nineteen

James

Awaking to hear Lucy screaming was one of the most terrifying sounds I had ever heard. I immediately jumped off the couch and ran into her room. There was a brief relief when I realised she wasn't hurt, it was just a nightmare.

Cato was pacing anxiously around the room as I sat on the bed next to her. I tried to shake her gently and call her name, but she didn't come round. I had to be more aggressive in the shakes to get her to come to.

The rage I felt on the inside threatened to boil over when she brought up the man from earlier. From what she told me, he sounded like he knew Amber personally. When we had worked out how to prove Anthony innocent, finding that man would be next on my list. He wasn't going to get away with hurting her.

I was grateful she asked me to stay. Truthfully, I was about to sleep on the floor just so I could keep an eye on her. The bed was a much more comfortable option. I soothed her hair as she fell asleep. I wasn't sure if I could sleep now, I was too worried about Lucy. Everything she was going through anybody else would have broken into pieces by now, but not Lucy. Lucy was the strongest person I had ever met. I stayed awake as long as I could to watch her, to make sure she didn't have any more nightmares. If she did, I would be right here to comfort her.

When morning came, it was time to brace the conversation with work. I would usually be in the office by now.

"Hey, Sandra, it's James. Is Michael free?"

"James who?" I almost scoffed.

I've worked there for months. I was slightly offended by how she didn't recognise my voice by now and I even referred to her by name.

"Weatherston." I listened to the clacking on her keyboard in the background.

"I can't find a case under Weatherston, is it under a different name?" *You've got to be fucking kidding me.*

"I'm not calling about a case, I'm a lawyer at the firm." I tried not to not show my annoyance in my voice.

"Oh, really?" Her voice sounded uninterested. Even with this snippet of information, she still didn't seem to know who I was. This conversation made me realise no matter what Michael would say, I made the right choice. What I was doing here with Lucy was important, *I was important.* "I'll put you through." I waited a beat.

"Michael Sawyer."

"Hey, Michael, it's James." I tried to keep the nerves away from my tone.

James

"James, where are you? You're an hour late and we need to go through the new witness statements." His voice was immediately harsh. It did make me wonder if I turned around and said I was in hospital, would he be kinder? Or would my absence continue to be nothing more than just an inconvenience for him?

"I had to go away for a few days." I could hear him huff on the other end of the phone. "Lucy was attacked, I needed to get her to safety." My words were originally met with silence. I waited for him to say something, feeling my impatience building with each second that passed.

"And you didn't think to fucking ask first?" Anger clouded his words.

"I'm sorry, it was an urgent situation. She was in *danger*." I tried to emphasise the last word, the importance of what I was doing.

"Were you following your mind or your dick on that decision?"

"What the fuck is that supposed to mean?" I was struggling to keep my cool. I shouldn't be talking to Michael that way, especially since I was already in his bad books. I knew exactly what he was insinuating, but I couldn't quite believe it. Lucy was a client, that was all. Okay, *maybe* we have gotten friendly over the past few days, but only because I was being supportive. I was just trying to give her a shoulder to cry on, not a dick to ride.

"Look, she's a pretty girl, even I can't deny that. I know I love the thought of sleeping with broken little Lucy, but is it worth your career?"

Did this guy just share his fantasy of sleeping with Lucy?

"You better take her name out of your mouth."

"Or what, Weatherston?" He was goading me and I knew it. I knew it and I still took the bait.

"You'll have trouble saying it with a broken jaw."

He laughed at me, *he fucking laughed at me*.

"James, we've all made bad mistakes because of beautiful women, so I'm going to let that slide." I could feel myself grinding my teeth.

"You know, I was going to put you on the Murray case with me. I wanted you sat at the trial with me. You're one of the most talented lawyers I've seen in recent years. It would be a shame to waste your potential."

My heart skipped a beat at his words. *He picked me*. All of my hard work over the past few months had been leading to this, to sit by his side and help him with this case. This would be a massive deal in my career. It could help me progress upwards and take on even more high-profile cases.

"If you aren't back here by Monday morning, not only are you off the case, you're fired, James." With those words, he hung up the phone, not even allowing me a chance to respond.

This was his ultimatum, how I responded would be my choice. Either I stayed here with Lucy, helping her with her father's case and lose everything I had worked for, or I went back to my job and lived as I had done for the past few months.

This Murray case was everything to me…or at least it used to be everything to me.

My priorities had changed.

Twenty

Lucy

When I woke up the bed was empty, neither James nor Cato were anywhere to be found. Looking at the clock, it was late morning. I don't remember the last time I slept that long. Walking out into the main living area, I couldn't see either of them. Feeling confused, I peered out of the window. James was throwing a ball in the water for Cato to fetch. I don't think Cato has even seen water like this before, but he was loving it. My eyes fell then to James who was laughing as Cato was splashing about in the lake. I wish I had a camera on hand to capture this moment, the pure joy on his face made me smile. I hadn't seen him smile like that before.

I opened up the front door and started walking towards them.

"What are you boys up to?" I shouted out as I approached. Both of their attentions turned to me. At first this was sweet, until a soaked Cato launched himself at me and knocked me to the ground .

"Cato!" I yelled out in between fits of laughter. I heard James' loud laugh get closer to me before he pulled me back up to my feet.

"Sorry, someone was excited to go in the water and I didn't want to wake you up." Even though I was now on my feet, he hadn't let go of my arm and I found myself naturally moving closer to him.

"He loves it." I watched as Cato ran back into the water. "Makes me wish I had brought an outfit to swim in."

"We can go into town and pick you something up, if you want."

"Really?"

"Of course. I was going to suggest going on a food run later, anyway. I know we have the case to work on, but you deserve some time to relax, as well." He paused. "It's okay to have a little fun. Besides, it's been months since I've been here. I'd love to show you around my hometown." The smile on his face was the cutest thing. He genuinely seemed so happy to be here. So much happier than I had seen him in the city. He seemed to be at peace here.

"What about your work?" I asked. In the rush of last night, I didn't even think about the fact James should be at work right now. He had told me that Michael was only letting him work my father's case outside of working hours, so he can't be pleased we are here.

"Oh, I called them this morning. It's all sorted."

"They are okay with you being here? What about the Murray case?" I was surprised by this.

"They understood that you were in danger and that I needed

to be here with you. They told me to take as long as I needed. There are plenty of other people who can work the Murray case."

"But I know how much you wanted to be on that case, you can't give that up for this."

"It's my choice, Lucy, and I am choosing to be here. There will be other cases and I can't keep you safe if I'm in the city."

I paused for a moment, taking in the gravity of what he was saying. Being here with me means he can't work on other cases. It was nice they were being accommodating for him, but I couldn't help feeling guilty, like I was impacting his dream. I wasn't worth him taking time off work.

"We can go back, James." I didn't particularly want to go back, but I wasn't going to let him throw this away. "Or maybe I could go to my aunt's like my mom did."

"No," he said sternly. He cleared his throat. "I mean, it's fine, Lucy; you're not forcing me to be here. I want to be here." He hesitated before continuing. "I want to be here with you." Selfishly, I enjoyed the sentiment. I don't think I had been someone's first choice or top priority before, but James was choosing me. He was choosing to work my father's case with me over everything else. I placed my hand on his arm and he smiled.

"Thank you for being here. I'm sorry about last night." Despite the beautiful day outside, there was still a part of me that lingered in the darkness of my nightmare. Still a part of me that wanted to constantly look over my shoulder in case the man came back. He wanted me dead—I couldn't be certain he wouldn't look for me.

"You don't have anything to be sorry about. My back was grateful to be off that couch," he said with a small wink. "Was your dream about what happened yesterday?" he asked as he moved in closer, his free hand now holding my waist. I nodded, but couldn't find the words.

It was hard to describe how I felt about James. As his hands touched me, I didn't feel nervous or shy. I don't have butterflies raging a war in my stomach. I feel completely and utterly calm in his presence. *I feel safe.*

"Do you believe in fate? That things always happen for a reason?" I asked. He was quiet at first, his eyes gazing down at me.

"Sometimes," he said after a beat. "On one side, there are so many good things that come about because of situations, giving you a clear reason as to why." A small smile flickered on his lips, his eyes not wavering. *Did he mean me?* "Then on the other hand, so many cruel things happen that make me think, what could possibly be the reason for all that pain?"

"Your sister…" I said softly. With those words, I had wiped any hint of a smile off his face and guilt consumed me.

"What reason could possibly be good enough for her death? What higher fucking purpose did all that serve?" He didn't raise his voice, but there was tension. "It tore everything apart; it ruined our lives and my parents have never been the same."

"Will you visit them whilst we are here?"

"I'm not sure, I don't know if they would even want to see me." There was a sadness in his tone.

"I can come with you? Maybe we could pop in and have a coffee with them whilst we are here. I'm sure they miss you."

"Maybe." He nodded. "But your father's case is the focus, I don't want to distract too much away from that."

I poked him playfully in the shoulder. "Weren't you the one who just said we needed to have a bit of fun whilst we were here?" His smile returned and I felt my shoulders loosen.

"I did, so we better go see about getting you something to swim in."

Twenty-One

James

Lucy seemed to push me out of my comfort zone in the best possible way. Everything came out so effortlessly when I was with her. Thoughts of Alice had been hidden away in my head for so long, but I wanted to tell Lucy everything about her. I wanted to tell her about how I was hurting; I knew she would make it better.

I felt guilty lying about my conversation with Michael, that the truth was I likely wouldn't have a job to go back to. Even working flat out all weekend, I couldn't guarantee we would have everything we needed to free Anthony, meaning I wouldn't make my ultimatum.

I meant what I said to Lucy, I was choosing her. I knew the stakes and it didn't matter.

I was willing to risk it all for Lucy Davis.

You would think with my impending unemployment I would feel worried, that I would be scared. I wasn't. Michael would damage my reputation, I knew that; he had connections and would make it hard for me to find another job. I knew if I could solve Anthony's case, if I could prove he was innocent, it would all be worth it. I would be able to prove that I was good enough, my name wouldn't be forgotten. *I would be important.*

I waited in the living room for Lucy to get ready, my mind wandering back to the case. From my last conversation with Anthony, I truly believed he was innocent.

He gave me an uneasy feeling, but I don't think it was related to Amber. There was something darker to him, something he wasn't telling me. I needed to talk to Vera, but she had skipped town. I hoped Lucy might have known her aunt's number, but I didn't want her to overhear the questions I asked. It was a careful balance of having to ask difficult questions whilst not upsetting the person I cared about. I was constantly reminding myself that this was her family, the people who, until a few days ago, were the closest thing to her. I know both of her parents' actions had caused a rift between them all. I don't know if Lucy would ever get over it, but even if she did, her entire life was going to change. No matter what happened, I was staying right by her side for as long as she'd let me.

"Is this a suitable outfit for wandering around the streets of Rosehaven?" Lucy re-entering the room broke my train of thought. She gave a twirl as she spoke. God she was beautiful.

"You'll fit right in," I said teasingly. That wasn't true at all. Lucy didn't fit in, Lucy stood out in the best possible way. As we got out of the car and walked into the store, that became more obvious to me. Nobody even came close to her. I watched her as we walked around the store, her eyes were darting everywhere. It took me a while to realise she was looking for *him*.

Till Death Parts Us

Other than when she explained the situation on the phone to me, we hadn't really discussed it. I felt guilty, like I completely brushed it all off.

Obviously, I took care of her after her nightmare, but we hadn't dealt with any of the feelings she was having. I could tell she was hurting before, but it was worse now. I observed her further as she placed things into the cart. Every single time, she looked over her shoulder.

The anger rose up inside of me again as it had yesterday. He was still out there, so she was still scared. It didn't matter that she felt safe with me, he was going to linger in the back of her mind. The only true way to make her feel safe was to find him and make sure he couldn't hurt her again. I needed to find out who he was, which was going to involve me asking her some difficult questions. I needed more details, I needed to know everything about the attack.

I wasn't going to push her today. Today was all about having fun, swimming in the lake, and just letting loose. There was no need to upset her with those questions now.

"James, do you…" Lucy began, but before she could finish, I was tackled to the floor. I squirmed, trying to turn myself over to fight off the attack.

"Did you think you could come into town and not tell me?" I immediately recognised Daines' voice as I rolled onto my back. I punched him in the shoulder as he helped me to my feet.

"You fucking asshole." Both of our eyes gravitated towards Lucy who looked terrified. I wanted to smack him round the face for scaring her. "It's okay, this is my friend, Daines." She seemed relieved; we had talked about Daines before and I felt better seeing her features calm.

James

"Your friend Daines who loves you and has missed you," he said as he embraced me, squeezing me tight.

"I missed you, too, but get off me." I laughed as I tried to fight against him.

"No, I have not been able to hug you for months. You are going to stand there and accept my love." I heard Lucy giggle behind me and I stopped fighting and hugged him back. He was dressed in full uniform, so I assumed he was on duty. I wondered what Lucy thought of him. He was a fairly toned man, but he was also an absolute dork.

"In my defence, I only got here last night. It was sort of a last-minute trip," I said as we pulled away.

"Are you going to introduce me to the gorgeous lady loading things into your shopping cart?" He raised his eyebrows at me before glancing at Lucy.

"This is Lucy." There was a brief look of recognition on his face, but he quickly changed his expression. I knew his opinion on me taking the case. I was slightly worried how he would feel about me hanging out with her and staying at the cabin.

"Jack Daines." He held out a hand and she took it. "I'm sorry I scared you. Weatherston is a slippery bastard when you get him, you just have to pin him down." Lucy laughed loudly, a twinge of jealousy came over me.

"James has told me about you," she said, looking over to me. I almost felt a little embarrassed. I may not have known Lucy long, but she was becoming a big part of my life. It was strange seeing two of the most important people to me meet.

"Everything he said is a lie," he said teasingly. "How long are you guys in town for?" Lucy looked at me to answer.

"A few days, at least. We are working a case so until we

make a breakthrough, we're staying at my dad's cabin." Daines nodded knowingly.

"Maybe we can have some dinner together, all of us. I'd love for you to meet Angie." I hesitated in responding to him. I didn't know how Lucy would feel about that and it felt too awkward to ask her in this moment.

"I'm not sure, we've got a lot of work to do." Daines looked disappointed and I couldn't help but feel guilty.

"What about tomorrow night?" Lucy interjected. "I'm happy to cook something."

"Perfect!" Daines' face lit up and I felt relief that Lucy came to my rescue. "I'll leave you two to it, but it was lovely to meet you, Lucy." I watched their interaction and felt happy. I wanted them to get on. Daines grabbed my face, turning it to the side before giving me a big, slobbery kiss on my cheek . "See you tomorrow, Weatherston."

I knew he was doing it on purpose to embarrass me in front of Lucy. He was such a dick. I couldn't wait to embarrass him ten times over tomorrow with Angie.

Twenty-Two

Lucy

I thought I was going to pass out on the spot when I watched James be tackled to the ground. It was only a brief moment, but as I saw the police officer on top of him, I felt panicked inside. Physically, on the outside, I was frozen still. I felt embarrassed that I didn't even move. I didn't protect James or run to help him. If roles were reversed, he wouldn't have hesitated.

I couldn't help it, the image of the police officer made me think of my father, of the way he was being treated. For a split second, I saw him being pushed to the ground by a police officer. The whole event motivated me to push harder to free my father. To find out who really killed Amber Jones. To get justice for both of them.

I felt calmer when James introduced Daines. We had spoken about him before and I could tell then how much Daines meant to him. It was also clear watching them interact how much

James meant to Daines, too. I laughed as I watched them interact, enjoying this side of James. I could tell he was a little embarrassed and he kept stealing quick glances my way. I felt honoured that he would even want to impress me. There was nothing embarrassing about the way they were acting, they were sweet. It made me wonder why James didn't come home more. He seemed so happy to be here.

I wasn't exactly sure why James hesitated on seeing Daines again, but it was clear that spending time with him made him seem happy. Selfishly, I also wanted to watch them interact more, maybe poke Daines for more info on James. I wanted to dig deeper into the kind man who was sacrificing everything for me.

"Are you okay? He's an ass for frightening you," James said after Daines walked off.

"I'm fine. It scared me at first, but he wasn't being malicious. Besides, he seems nice."

We headed towards the checkout after I grabbed a few more things for tomorrow night's dinner. "How long have he and Angie been together?"

"About six months, I think. Maybe more."

"And you haven't met her? The two of you seem so close." I thought back to Daines' comment about not having hugged him in months.

"I haven't been home in about a year," James admitted.

"How does it feel to be back home again?" Despite my current circumstances, I couldn't imagine not seeing my family for that long, or any of my friends. Especially if I had a friend that I was close to like he was with Daines.

"It feels like exactly where I'm supposed to be," he said with a sigh. "And I'm a little angry at myself that I didn't see that until now."

I pondered his words for a while as we completed our other errands. We both got swimming costumes for later and headed back to the cabin. It felt weirdly normal to be out running errands together. I almost forgot that we were fundamentally just a lawyer and client. We had definitely crossed a lot of lines even being friendly to each other.

I took in the sights of Rosehaven as we drove around—it was a pretty little town. Nothing like the city of Kirston at all. People here seemed happy, they were friendly with one another. I watched as people who recognised James asked him about his life. He seemed like he was at home here, despite not having been back in a year.

People also seemed happy to see him and I watched him thrive as he spoke to everybody. No matter who they were, he always immediately introduced me to them whilst telling me their connection to him. He spoke to all of them the same, like he was happy to see them. We passed teachers, old high school friends, and neighbours. James was clearly popular in the town and it made me wonder once more why he hadn't been back.

When he introduced me each time, he didn't refer to me as his client. *This is my friend, Lucy.* He would beam at me each time he said it and I felt my heart soar. He was excited to introduce me to these people. He never mentioned my father or any of the negatives about my life, but he spoke about me proudly.

Lucy is studying for a business qualification in college.
Lucy used to run track when she was younger.
You competed at nationals for dance, too, didn't you, Lucy?
At first, I wondered how he knew all this information about

me. *Had he been researching me?* Then I realised I told him all my childhood stories when we had dinner. I wittered on for hours about all the silly little things when he was getting a back story about my father. *He remembered everything.*

I knew at the time he was listening to me, but I thought he was focused on my father's role in my childhood. I didn't realise the whole time he was also listening in such detail about *me*. Every time he said something new about me, I found myself getting teary. I had never experienced this before and I didn't know how to process having someone care like this.

Eventually, we drove back to the cabin ready to start our afternoon in the water. I was excited to spend some time learning more about James. He had taken the time to know so much about me. I wanted to spend any free time outside the case getting to know him.

"You know, you said this place was exactly where you were supposed to be?" I asked as we pulled up the cabin.

"Yeah?" he questioned.

"I think it's exactly where I am supposed to be, too."

Twenty-Three

James

I couldn't wipe the smile off my face all morning as we ran errands around my hometown. I hadn't felt this good in the longest time. It had been a long time since I had walked the high street, but it felt like I had never left. I realised that in the city I never truly felt like I was settled, but here I knew I belonged.

After Daines left, I passed several people that knew me or that I had grown up with. Each one talked to me like it was only yesterday they saw me. They remembered things about me that even I had forgotten. People really knew who I was here. I'd been missing that small town feeling; everyone knowing everyone wasn't always a bad thing. In this case, it made me feel wanted.

We headed back to the cabin after our town run and I was secretly excited to get some alone time with Lucy. I enjoyed catching up with familiar people, but I had been desperate to spend more time with her.

Today wasn't about me, today was about her. I wanted to spend the day making her forget about everything, just letting loose and having fun in the water.

Cato bolted straight out the door when we got back and flung himself into the water. I think he agreed with Lucy's sentiment in the car.

I think it's exactly where I am supposed to be, too.

Her words dangled in my head as I unloaded the car before heading out towards one of the row boats tied up by the lake. It had seen better days, but there were no holes in it. It wouldn't exactly be the best first experience for Lucy if it started sinking five minutes in.

"I made us some lunch to take," Lucy said as she approached me. "Are we all good to go?"

"Just got a couple more things to load up, boss, and then we are ready." She laughed. "You think Cato will stay in this?" I asked with a raised eyebrow. I had planned to row us out to a little island in the middle of the lake to spend the afternoon. I was slightly worried a certain four-legged friend might jump ship.

"I'll keep hold of him, I promise." I finished my final checks and loaded our stuff in before offering a hand to Lucy to help her in. After helping her in, Cato jumped in behind her, shaking the boat. I stifled a laugh as he nearly capsized the boat.

"You sure you want to bring him?" I teased as I climbed into the boat.

"He'll be fine." She giggled. "Besides, we can't exclude him from this little family day out, can we?"

Little family day out. The words clung to me as I started to

James

row. She was likely only making a joke, but that was a little bit how it felt. Everything about this day felt completely and utterly normal. Despite the circumstances, we were having a good day together and everything in the world was peaceful for just one day. I had almost forgotten about all the drama with work and the case. I had let myself get completely lost in being with Lucy.

We had two sets of oars, but I told Lucy to just relax and take in the view. I had been in this lake hundreds of times and it never stopped being beautiful. Despite this, the only thing I looked at whilst rowing was Lucy. No view could take my breath away quite like she could. I watched as she took in her surroundings, joy overcoming her face.

When we finally got to the little island, I hopped out first so I could tie it down, holding it as steady as I could so she could climb out. When she did and we had unloaded, she took my hand and started to pull me up the hill. I let myself go willingly, grateful to have her touch.

"This spot looks perfect," she squealed as she let go to get the picnic blanket out. "Look at this view!" She could hardly contain the excitement in her voice as she looked around. I looked around.

I'd been here hundreds of times. Mostly, we came here as teenagers to drink some beers, but it was beautiful. Still, it wasn't what I wanted to look at as my gaze returned to her.

We sat down on the blanket; it wasn't lost on me how close she was sitting. She had definitely gone overboard on the picnic she prepared, but I wasn't going to crush her enjoyment. This was all about her.

"If we are eating like this every day, I'm going to gain like twenty pounds this weekend," I teased as she continued to pull food out of the bag.

"You just wait for what I have planned to eat tomorrow night. I'm a feeder, I can't help it."

"I can't wait," I said, dropping the teasing tone. "So, you like to cook?"

"I love it." Her face lit up once more. "I always wanted to do family dinners, but with my father's shifts, we rarely all ate at the same time. So the food I made became leftovers for him to have later." There was a hint of sadness in her tone.

"Well, you can cook for me any time," I said in an attempt to lighten the mood again. "I've basically been living off frozen dinners since moving out." Lucy gasped mockingly.

"No more frozen dinners for you while I'm around!" she said sternly. "You'll be eating some proper home cooked meals for the next few days." *I couldn't wait.*

We were quiet for a bit as we dug into the food. I don't think I realised how hungry I was until I started eating. I made it through an impressive amount of food.

"You know, I've always wanted to live in a small town like this," Lucy said once we had finished eating. We both laid down on the blanket, our eyes on the sky as we shuffled close to each other.

"Really? I took you to be a city girl."

"How dare you, Weatherston," she said, pretending to be annoyed. "No, I've always dreamed about moving somewhere like this. Having a family, a table full of kids to feed and love on." I could imagine Lucy as a mother. She had the right temperament for it. Even through everything that was happening, she remained calm. She handled everything with such grace.

"My mother was a bit like that when we were younger. Now

James

I'm an asshole adult who never shows up for those dinners."

"I wouldn't let them do that," she said determinedly. "Even as adults, I'd be making those kids come spend one night a week at mine for dinner. It's non-negotiable." That was another reason she would make an amazing mother. She was tenacious.

"Will you still come with me to see my parents? I was thinking on Sunday?" I had been thinking about them since we spoke about it earlier. It was unfair that I was keeping my parents at arm's length.

"I'll be there to hold your hand," she said as she turned to cuddle into me, her hand on my chest. "We're in this together, remember?"

I smiled. "Every step of the way."

"Every step of the way," she mused.

Twenty-Four

Lucy

After all the talk about children, I couldn't help but picture James as a father. I allowed that fantasy to consume my mind in a brief moment of quiet. One of the first things I noticed about him was how kind he was. Kids deserved a father who was kind. Until recently, I thought I had a father who was kind. Now I realised I was wrapped up in a lie. Call me naïve, but I didn't think James' kindness was a lie. I thought that about him before we got close, but he had no reason to lie to me then. He had no reason to pretend to be something he's not.

I bet he would be a really fun dad, too. He was always cracking jokes and teasing me. From seeing him briefly interacting with Daines, I could tell he was a bit of a prankster, too. That was a good quality to have.

Alongside this, he seemed protective and caring for those close to him. I had witnessed this firsthand and it made me

Lucy

feel happy that I was considered close enough to him to be protected by him. I was safe with James, I never wanted to leave his safety net he had built around me.

"How did you remember all those stories that I told you about my childhood?" I asked him as I leant on his chest.

"Because those stories mattered to me," he said without hesitation. "I like knowing these things about you."

"I want to know things about you, too." My voice came out a little bit whiny, making him laugh. I could feel his heartbeat against my ear. It was steady, just like how he made me feel.

"Ask away."

"How did you and Daines meet?"

"His parents moved to town just before first grade. I noticed him sitting on his own and, I don't know…it sounds stupid, but I was just kind of drawn to him. We have pretty much been inseparable since."

"So why don't you come back to visit much?" I felt almost cruel asking this question. It was deeply personal, but James and I were getting to the stage now where very little was off limits. He knew me at my worst, I wasn't exactly going to judge him.

He sighed before answering. "I feel like I carry this weight around with me everywhere I go, like this immense pressure that sits on my shoulders. I started to feel it the day after Alice died. Before she passed, she was the golden child. My sister was everything I wasn't. Please don't get me wrong, I don't mean that in a jealous way," he said defensively.

"She just always seemed to get everything right. My parents were obsessed with her. When I woke up in the hospital and saw their faces, I couldn't help but think that they were angry that I lived and she died."

117

"James, I'm sure that's not true." It was awful hearing his words, I could tell he believed in what he was saying. He genuinely thought his parents would rather he was dead than his sister.

"You don't see their faces every time they see me; I will always be a disappointment to them. *Always.* That's why I don't come home, I can't face their disappointment."

"How can they be disappointed in you? Look at you building your career. You're a lawyer, for fuck's sake. You are kind, you're funny, and you always put everyone else first. They should be proud of you; I know I'm proud of you." His eyes turned to face me and I could see there were tears in them.

"You know when they call me, they never ask if I'm okay or anything about my life? All they ask about is the cases I'm working on. Until I met you, the only person who ever cared was Daines." Seeing James this vulnerable broke my heart and I was about ready to give his parents a piece of my mind on Sunday. Right after I give Daines the biggest hug tomorrow for taking care of James.

"We can't control what others do and how they behave, that seems to be a lesson I'm learning. I can promise that I will always be interested in whether you're okay and what you are up to." I brought my hand up to his face, brushing lightly as I spoke.

"As much as I struggle with the concept of everything happens for a reason, I know there is a reason I met you," he whispered. I felt tears brimming in my own eyes. This had been exactly how I was feeling, but I hadn't been brave enough to say it out loud.

"I think so, too," was all I managed as we looked at each other for a moment.

Lucy

"I think I've been stopping myself from enjoying life." He moved to a sitting position and I followed suit, continuing to lean in close to him as he wrapped his arms around me. "Alice died and I lived. I've always felt guilty for that."

"You're exactly right, James. *You* lived. So you know what you need to do?" He looked at me with a raised brow. *"Live."*

I watched his facial expression change; he was deep in thought for a moment. After a pause, I noticed a smirk on his face. I hadn't known James Weatherston long, but I knew a smirk like that could only mean one thing. *Trouble*.

"You're right. Has your food gone down enough?"

"Yes…why?" I asked, raising a brow.

"Race ya!" He laughed as he stood up, took off his shirt, and started to run towards the water. "Last one there has to row us back!"

"That's not fair!" I shouted as I stood up, frantically trying to lift my dress over my head as I ran towards him. He beat me into the water, obviously, jumping off the deck with a splash. When I finally got my dress off, I jumped in behind him. "Asshole!" I splashed him as he got closer to me.

"You're the one who told me to live," he teased as he came closer to me. His arms wrapped around my waist, holding me afloat.

"Are you being sweet or are you about to dunk me in the water?"

"Well, I *was* being sweet, but now you've said that, I really want to dunk you in the water."

"Weatherston don't you…" I didn't get to finish my sentence as he dunked me in the water with a laugh. Even his dunking me in the water was done with gentleness, I could tell. It didn't stop me immediately seeking revenge when I came up by pushing him down. What followed next was slightly chaotic as we both tried to one up the other, all while Cato tried to fight his way into the mix. Eventually, we both got tired and came up for air. James' hands wrapped around me once more.

"You are trouble, James Weatherston," I teased as I put my hands around his neck.

"That's funny, because I was going to say the same thing about you, boss," he said, the cheeky smirk coming back to his face.

"Maybe we can be trouble together?" I shot back as his eyes met mine. I leant up and kissed him. I could tell he was surprised at first, but he quickly began to kiss me back. He pulled me in tighter, holding me as close to him as he possibly could. Everything about this felt exactly right.

Twenty-Five

James

I wasn't expecting Lucy to kiss me, but I didn't hesitate to kiss her back. I had been thinking about it all day. Hell, I had been thinking about it since we first met.

"This is probably a bad idea," she said, looking at me as we broke off the initial kiss.

"A terrible one," I agreed, going back to kissing her again. We all needed to give in to a bad idea every now and then. I didn't think about my career or the case. I didn't care about any of it at the moment. The only thing I cared about was being close to her. It didn't matter what I needed to sacrifice to keep Lucy, I would do it.

I kept my hands moving between her waist and her back. I wanted Lucy to set the tone, given everything she has been through. I wasn't going to push her further until she was ready. We were quiet for a beat when we finally pulled away. It wasn't awkward, we were just enjoying being in each other's presence.

"How about a swimming race?" she asked, making me laugh.

"You know I literally grew up on this water, right? Are you sure you want to race me?"

"What, are you scared, Weatherston?" God, I couldn't even begin to describe the way her teasing me made me feel.

"Only scared of upsetting you when I win." She looked at me, her smile bright with a hint of mischievousness in it.

"From here to there?" she asked, pointing to a rock in the distance. With a nod, we were off. I was potentially too over confident, because when I came up for air, I could see her ahead of me. I guess this is why she had suggested it. *Game on, Lucy Davis.*

I gave it everything I had, but she just beat me to the post. She came up out of the water with the brightest smile I had ever seen from her. I hoped her struggles were truly in the back of her mind.

"I let you win," I lied, my pride kicking in.

"You did not!" Her voice raised in a jovial tone. "I saw you fighting for your life trying to keep up with me." She hit my arm playfully. "I've always been a good swimmer."

"You definitely hustled me; I don't remember you mentioning swimming in a single one of your stories." She rolled her eyes at me.

We spent the rest of the afternoon messing about in the water. There were plenty more races in which I lost every single one. Turns out Lucy also competed in swimming, too. *What can't she do?*

I felt like a kid again when I was with her, in the best possible way. I felt like I could completely be myself around her and just let everything else go. We didn't talk about any of the

James

bad stuff when we were in the water. We dove into more childhood stories from both sides. I told her all about how my friends and I would spend summers and weekends out on the water. After recovering from the crash, I liked to come swimming on my own, too. I struggled a lot to do physical activities I had previously enjoyed before. I would come here and swim around the lake; the weightlessness helped me gain some strength back in my body.

At the time, I was embarrassed by it. I didn't want my friends to see how much I was struggling to recover from the crash, both physically and mentally. I didn't want them to see how broken I was. So, I never told anyone that I was coming up here to swim, that swimming was basically the only thing that stopped me falling into a dark place that I wouldn't be able to get out of. Until now, that was. Until Lucy. I liked telling her things about my life, I wanted her to really know me. The real me.

Despite the fact she lost the earlier race, I did row us back to the cabin. Lucy sat sleepily on the other side of the boat with Cato laying on her. We dragged ourselves back inside and finished off the picnic; neither of us had the energy to cook this evening. We hadn't kissed since earlier in the day, but we seemed to steal touches wherever we could.

As much as I wanted to be with her or near her, I couldn't shake the anxious feeling in the back of my head. My mind wandered to my conversation with Michael, the way he looked down on the idea of a lawyer falling for a client or someone related to the case. He wasn't wrong. It was frowned upon and if people found out, it could ruin me. Especially since I was about to get fired for skipping out on the Murray case. I was running the risk here of never being hired in my profession again.

Was I being a fool? I didn't feel particularly foolish. No part of me regretted any of the actions I was taking. Still, I felt like I should have regrets. I was potentially giving up on everything for a girl I'd met a few days ago. A girl with a life that was messy and falling apart.

That was the problem, though. Lucy wasn't just a girl. Not to me, anyway. To me, Lucy was everything I'd ever wanted. She was brave, selfless, and funny. She gave me a run for my money. Alongside that, she was hands down the most beautiful woman I had ever seen. I had noticed her the second she walked into the office, and in different circumstances, I would have been asking her out straight away. My professional side had been winning up until now. Now, I had nothing to lose and everything to gain by pursuing Lucy.

There was still the complication of her father's case. I did believe he was innocent of killing Amber—and that wasn't just because I had feelings for Lucy. The motive the police were trying to give him didn't make sense. He was about to start a whole new life with her, why would he then strangle her to death? It just didn't make sense. I really didn't think he was lying about Amber. I don't feel like he is the perfect person Lucy paints him to be, but I don't think he killed a woman he loved.

Truthfully, I didn't know if I would be able to free Anthony. Proving his innocence was going to be near impossible. Everything was circumstantial, some fingerprints and no sign of anyone else being there, but it played in the prosecution's favour, not mine. I'd seen people prosecuted on less evidence. Kirkston was always desperate to imprison a suspect, even if there was a chance the person was innocent. They needed

James

that conviction.

As I showered off the day, I wondered what Lucy's feelings for me were. Was I just a way to escape everything she had going on? She might have just been looking for something casual as a distraction and I just happened to be nearby. It didn't feel like that, though. It felt like there was more to it.

Would the outcome of her father's case change how she felt about me? If I wasn't able to prove his innocence, would she want to still be with me? Or would she completely cut ties because being around me would haunt her? If I failed to free him, I would risk losing the only thing I really wanted.

I already felt like a failure to my parents and my work. I didn't want to feel like one to Lucy, too.

When I left the bathroom, Lucy was sitting on the bed. We hadn't had the conversation about sleeping arrangements since we shared a bed last night. I had only laid with her because she was having nightmares. I wanted to be close to her in case that happened again tonight, I wanted to be there to comfort her. I also didn't want to assume she was comfortable with me here. The kiss complicated things, the dynamic between us was changing.

"Will you stay with me again tonight? I don't want to be on my own." Her words filled me with both relief and sadness. Relief that I didn't have to bring up the conversation, she *wanted* me here. At the same time, I felt sad that she was scared enough to need me to comfort her.

"Of course," I said, climbing into bed next to her. Instinctively, my arms were around her and shuffled close to me.

"Thank you for today," she said, gazing up at me. "I had the best day."

"Me, too." I lifted her chin and brought my lips to hers.

Despite the fact she had initiated the kiss earlier, I was still surprised by the eagerness in the way she returned mine. There was a tenderness and intimacy to it that I had never experienced before, which only left me wanting more. I regained control and we pulled away. I wasn't going to push for more, not with everything else going on.

"Goodnight, Weatherston." I could tell she felt the same as she cuddled into me.

"Night, boss."

Twenty-Six

Lucy

I had the nightmare again.

Even as I woke up with James holding me close, I couldn't shake the feeling of the hands around my throat. I couldn't make the sight of his dark eyes disappear as he tried to take my life. I wondered how it felt to take someone's life, to stand over them and watch their life fade from their eyes. The thought made me shudder.

Did he enjoy it? Was there a pleasure that people took from killing? I couldn't imagine it as a pleasurable experience, but then again, I had never imagined killing someone before. I thought about it now, having my hands around someone's neck. That feeling of pressing down hard as they struggled underneath you. I think I would need to drug someone to do it, too. I would struggle enough with the potential hesitation, but I wouldn't want to risk them overpowering me. Giving them sleeping medication would actually be a clever idea.

I'm smaller so I would need that advantage. I pictured the man's dark eyes as if our roles were reversed. I shook the thought from my brain, for a moment I was scared of myself. It didn't matter that this man had hurt me, wouldn't I be just as bad if I went after him? Could killing ever be excusable? Just because he tried to kill me, it didn't necessarily mean he deserved to die.

Trying to distract myself from my mixed feelings, I thought again about Amber Jones. If we went along the train of my thought that my father did it, I didn't understand why my father would drug her. He's six foot three and of a larger build. Amber looked roughly around my size at five foot six. A man of my father's size could easily overpower her. Whoever killed Amber must have been worried about her fighting back, so they resorted to drugging her. By that logic, that had to be someone of a similar size to Amber or maybe someone with a physical weakness who was worried about her fighting back.

I made a note to ask James his opinion on this. We had agreed to work on the case tomorrow after our fun day at the lake. We had work to do, and as much as I wanted to enjoy my time with James, we were here for a reason. I would be lying if I said I wasn't looking forward to taking a break in the evening with Daines and Angie. I imagine it'll be welcome after going through files all day.

When I had my nightmare, James was immediately there. He stroked my hair and whispered comforting words as he calmed me down. He had fallen back asleep now, but I still felt calmer being by his side.

Yesterday meant everything to me in a way I struggle to express. I needed a day to forget about all the darkness that was surrounding my life. Everyone who I thought cared about

Lucy

me had seemingly abandoned me. Even before we left, my mother hadn't called once to check on me and neither had any of my friends.

James was new to my life, but he was the only consistent thing. He took care of me in a way no one else had before and I found myself wanting to cling to him. Part of me was worried I was becoming too dependent on him; maybe my neediness would suffocate him. The truth was he was the only light I had in situations where everything else was dark. I desperately needed his light to will me to keep going.

It crossed my mind briefly that he may have been using my vulnerability as a way to get what he wanted out of me. I was in a weak position, feeling lonely, and we were alone together in a cabin. He could easily take advantage of me. This thought didn't stay for long.

His actions spoke louder than that fleeting thought. From the moment he met me, he had always been gentle with me. Even today when we were roughhousing in the lake, he did it with such care. His gentleness helped me feel secure around him, I knew he wouldn't hurt me. There was a level of care shared between us that went deeper than my insecurities. They wiped away all the doubt I had about going into something like this.

It was a terrible idea to date the lawyer who was taking on my father's case, probably one of the worst ones I have ever had. Was that going to stop me? Absolutely not.

Things between us were complicated, I felt that everything was hanging in the balance whilst this case lingered. I was letting myself get distracted with James, but I couldn't help it. I hadn't forgotten about my father or the case, how could I? I was just trying to find some joy in the moments in between.

Did that make me a bad person?

In the quiet of the night, I thought about what my life was going to be like after this was all over. There were two possible endings in my mind and truthfully, I was planning for both.

The first ending was that my father would be found guilty, either because he was or because we couldn't prove his innocence. This felt like a hard one to swallow, especially the latter. He would spend the rest of his life in prison and he would hardly be a part of my life anymore. If I got married or had kids, he wouldn't be there for any of it. If he was guilty, he deserved that ending. If he wasn't, then I would have to live with my own guilt my entire life. The guilt that I couldn't help him.

If James and I's relationship progressed into more, would we be able to survive that?

Of course there was the other ending, that we did prove my father's innocence and he was free. My parents' relationship was over and the split was going to be messy. Alongside that, he was going to abandon us for Amber without so much as a second thought. Is that something I would be able to forgive?

I knew in my heart I never wanted to live in my family home again. The walls were filled with memories that I didn't want at the forefront of my mind anymore. Memories of a happy family that I am not sure ever really existed.

No matter what happened between James and I, I knew I had to move away. I meant it when I said Rosehaven felt exactly where I was supposed to be.

My home was broken and I was ready to find a new one.

Twenty-Seven

James

I decided to surprise Lucy by making us some breakfast. I didn't cook for myself at home, but that didn't mean I didn't know how to. It felt kind of sad just to cook for yourself. It added to the loneliness I would often feel in the evenings, so I stopped doing it.

When I was younger, I used to love cooking with my mother. I always used to watch her make my father home cooked meals. I guess you could say we had a traditional family; my mother stayed at home and my father went to work. As much as I enjoyed Lucy's cooking, I wanted more than that for whatever this was between us. I wanted her to feel like I could look after her, like I wouldn't rely on her for everything. Whatever happened we would be a partnership, we were in this together.

Lucy wandered out of the bedroom just as I was plating up the eggs.

"I'm sorry, is James Weatherston, the fancy pants lawyer,

making me breakfast?" she asked mockingly. "You are full of surprises," she said, planting a kiss on my cheek as she walked over to grab a drink.

"I'll happily eat both of these plates if you're going to give me cheek."

"No!" she said, panicked. "It smells so good, don't take this away from me." I carried them both over to the table as she sat across from me. "What prompted this?"

"No reason, I just figured you'd probably kick me out of the kitchen if I tried to help with dinner later, so I could at least make breakfast." She laughed.

"You are one hundred percent correct; I absolutely hate people hovering over me when I'm cooking. You can stay far away from me later."

"Unfortunately, Lucy, I struggle to stay away from you." Her cheeks flushed at my comment and I smirked.

"So, what is the plan of action for today?"

She may have changed the subject, but I could still see the rose tint on her cheeks.

"Well, I need to review everything I've got, but I think it would be a good idea to start throwing out theories we can work on as well."

"What kind of theories?"

"Of who killed Amber Jones. Finding the killer is obviously a sure-fire way of proving your father's innocence. We also need to figure out more about your father's whereabouts that evening. There is a difference between the statements your mother gave and your father."

"I'd forgotten about that."

"Your father says he was home and in bed by ten-thirty, but your mother says he didn't get in till after midnight."

James

"So, one of them is lying."

It wasn't a question she was making, but a statement. I hadn't discussed these parts of the files with her yet in depth, but I couldn't hide it. She needed to know exactly what we were up against.

"We need to figure out who and why out of the two of them. If your father lied, then we have to consider the possibility he is guilty. If your mother lied, we need to know why. She might have just done it out of spite." As much as I wanted to protect Lucy's feelings, the longer this went on, the more I realised there was no protecting her from this. This was her family, after all. Her input was vital.

"Who do you think is lying?"

"Your mother," I said without hesitating. I'm not sure if it was more that I thought she was lying or I wanted her to be the one who was lying. Vera being the one who was lying made it a lot easier for me—we would have more of an alibi to work with. It wasn't foolproof, but it was better than what we had.

"I hope she's the one lying," Lucy said with a sigh. "I would hate to go through all this and he was guilty the whole time."

"I don't think your father killed Amber. I'm not saying he isn't hiding secrets, but I don't think killing her is one of them."

"You think he's hiding secrets? What secrets?" I regretted saying that part out loud.

I was trying to hide as much negativity about her father from me as I could. The truth was, I didn't like him and I certainly didn't trust him.

"I just get the impression he isn't saying everything on his mind, that's all. I don't think it is anything that will affect the case."

"I guess he was hiding a whole other life from me, so it wouldn't be much of a surprise." I reached out and grabbed her hand, rubbing it softly with my thumb.

"No matter which way this goes, I'm here for you." She smiled and squeezed my hand.

"So, what do we do to find out who is lying?"

"I have a plan," I said with a little smirk.

"I'm listening," she said, raising her brow questioningly at me.

"I think we should pretend that you're still at home and don't let her know that we've grown…" I paused, "*Close.*"

"Pretend we have a normal lawyer-client relationship, you mean? Act like you're not obsessed with me?" she asked teasingly. *I wasn't going to deny it, I was obsessed with her.*

"Exactly that," I said with a smirk. "I think you should call her, try to find out what she remembers from that night. Just pretend it's been bothering you and we can see if she deviates from what she told the police. She won't necessarily know that you know her statement if we play it like I haven't involved you in the case at all."

"So, you want me to act like I know absolutely nothing?"

"Yeah, then once I know what she said to you, I'll call her separately on Monday so she doesn't get suspicious. We'll have to use a phone booth for yours in case your aunt has called ID on her landline. There's one outside of town we can use where it'll be quiet."

"You want to do this today?" I nodded.

"As much distance as we can put between our calls without waiting too long, the better. Are you up for that?" I suddenly felt guilty, like I was putting a lot of pressure on her. I had unknowingly switched into work mode. She gave me a nod

James

and a small smile.

"Thank you," I said, squeezing her hand in an attempt to reassure her. "I do have one more thing I wanted to talk to you about." She looked nervous as her expression willed me to continue. "I wanted to ask Daines for his help on the case."

"Help with what?" I could hear how reluctant she was by her tone.

"Well, he knows who you are and what my connection to you is. I called him when I first took it on for his advice." She moved her hand away from mine and I felt an emptiness at the absence of her touch. "We had only really just met then, I'm sorry. Otherwise, I would have asked your permission first." She was silent as she looked at me. I didn't ever want Lucy to be upset with me.

"Daines has connections within the force, I think he might be able to get me some insider information. I trust him with my entire life, I promise you he will have our best interests at heart."

"*Our?*" She reached her hand out to me again and I breathed a sigh of relief.

"Yes, boss, *our*." Her gaze met mine and a smile formed on her lips. "We are a team, Lucy. I want you to help us get through this. I want to give you the resolution to all this so we can have a future."

"Well, I guess I better call my mother then, eh?"

Twenty-Eight

Lucy

My mind was all over the place after breakfast with James. I wanted to focus on the fact he referred to them as our interests, he was thinking about my future. *Our future.* I wished I could sit and enjoy that concept, but my mind was flooded with something else: the phone call with my mother.

I trusted James and was happy to go with whatever plan he came up with, but I was dreading talking to her. I couldn't shake the feeling that she abandoned me, yet here I was, having to reach out to her. If we were going to prove she was lying, I'd have to be nice to her—at least until she told me her side of the story.

I was slow to shower and get dressed, trying to prolong the morning as much as possible. My head ran through all of the things I needed to say to her. I needed to know how much she knew about my father's affair, how much the two of them

Lucy

were hiding from me.

I didn't get the sense that my father had anything to hide; I felt like he had told me everything when we went to see him. I didn't understand why James felt there was more, but maybe I was just too close to it. Maybe I was just a naïve little girl.

My mother, however, had acted strangely before she left. I remembered her words telling me to make sure I told the truth about my father. What truth was she referring to? It had bugged me ever since she said it. It made me feel like I was stupid, that there was something right in front of my face I was missing. A sign I should have seen this whole time.

"Ready, boss?" James seemed nervous as he waited for me by the door. I could tell he was feeling guilty for suggesting this call.

"Ready as I'll ever be," I said with a shrug.

"If you don't want to, we can come up with another plan." His hands found their way to my hips as he pulled me close, leaning his forehead against mine. For a brief moment, I forgot about everything else.

"It's a good plan, I'm just really nervous," I said, bringing my hands up to his shoulders. "The whole dynamic between my mother and I has changed. I feel like so much has changed in such a short time."

"Any good changes?" he asked with a small laugh.

"*One* good change, but I think you know what that is," I teased. He moved his head, planting a soft kiss on my lips.

"You've had a lot you've had to deal with in such a short time. You're dealing with this all incredibly, Lucy. You should be proud of yourself." His words always had a way of making me feel better.

I think sometimes I forget exactly how everything has

changed. I forget that just over a week ago I had parents who loved me and each other. I was in college studying towards my degree with dreams of starting up my own business or maybe working towards management in a company. I had goals and ambitions. I thought one day I would get married, have kids, and watch my parents slide straight into a grandparent's role. I had always looked to my parents to be the example of what a loving relationship should be. How wrong I had been.

Now I am here and everything I knew about them was a lie. My parents were not happy and apparently hadn't been for a long time. My father was having affairs and insinuated my mother was, too. They spent their time sneaking around, and when they were with me, I just had these fake versions of who they were. Now was the time to find out who they really were and make sure I never became either of them.

James drove us out to the phone booth on the edge of town. There were a few people walking past, but it was fairly quiet. Even if they overheard, the context would be lost on them.

"I'll stand nearby, but if you want me to leave at any point, I'll go back to the car. Just give me a nod." I was going to say the whole thing with him near, anyway, but I appreciated the respect he was giving me. I gave him a small smile before dialling my aunt's number. Luckily, I had the foresight to write it down and take it with me in case I needed to reach my mother.

My aunt picked up on the second ring.

"Hey, it's Lucy. Is Mom there?" I tried to hide my nerves from my voice. Part of me hoped she wasn't home. I heard my aunt call for my mother as we made brief and polite conversation. We didn't see much of my extended family and truthfully, I wasn't really in the mood for small talk.

Lucy

"Lucy, sweetheart!" My mother's voice came through bright and bubbly on the other side of the phone. Immediately, I felt my guard go up and the happiness in her voice. It felt unnatural for the circumstances. Everything that happened with my father aside, she hadn't even called me. Yet, she was sounding like she was living her best life. One that didn't include me.

"Hey, how are you?" I mustered up the happiest voice I could to respond.

"Great, we went shopping yesterday. It's so beautiful here, we might head down to the beach later on."

"That sounds great," I said through gritted teeth. "Have you heard much from the police?" It wasn't lost on me that she had yet to ask how I was.

"Not much since we made our statements." Her tone of voice dropped. "Apparently, your father will have a trial date soon." I looked over at James even though he couldn't hear what she said. I didn't want to have to face this trial. "Have you seen your father?" she asked reluctantly. I couldn't tell if she was just being nosy or if she actually cared.

"Not really. I saw him when we made our statements and once more to introduce him to the lawyer."

"Oh, the lawyer! I forgot about that, how is that all going?"

"I don't really know, I haven't had much contact with him. Dad's lawyer is pretty abrasive." I gave James an apologetic look. "I assume he mostly talks to Dad; I haven't heard from him since we saw Dad together." I didn't like lying to my mother.

"All lawyers tend to be assholes, I wouldn't worry. They work for the highest paycheck; they don't usually care whether someone is innocent or guilty."

Till Death Parts Us

"He's pro-bono, he's not earning anything from this or from us." I couldn't help but stand up for James even though I was supposed to pretend like I hardly knew him.

"I know that, but think of all the publicity he will get for working this. Even *when* your father gets his guilty charge, that man will be in all the papers. He'll probably have people knocking down the door to hire him, regardless." I hadn't really thought about the publicity side of things in all of this. Of course, I'd had reporters coming after me, but when people found out James was Dad's lawyer, they would press him, too. I wonder if he'd already been contacted for statements. I had been keeping an eye on the paper, but there had been nothing about him yet. If he was in it for the publicity, he would already be all over the news. Instead, he took me away from all the noise, somewhere safe and quiet.

"*If* Dad gets a guilty charge," I corrected her.

"Lou, your father is guilty," she said, sighing.

"How are you so sure? What happened that night?" This was what we were building towards, to try to catch her out.

"Your father has never been a good man, Lucy." *Liar, she's a fucking liar.* "I don't know for sure, but I know my own instincts, and my instinct tells me he killed Amber Jones."

"And mine tells me he didn't," I spat back.

"That's because you're a naïve little girl." Her tone was harsh. "You've always believed that the sun shone from your father, you never saw the truth." She was shouting now and I felt scared. Scared that I was going to lose both of them. "He has always been a monster; it just took this long for the truth to come out."

My mind went back to when the police officer came to tell us he'd be arrested. *I knew it*, she repeated over and over again.

Lucy

What did she know? What wasn't she telling me?

"If you knew that, why were you still with him?" The words that were in my head that night came to light now. I had nothing to lose anymore, all I wanted was the truth.

"We were safer with him then we were without him." Her voice was cold. "Everything I ever did was to protect you." I saw red at that moment.

"Protect me? Mom, you *abandoned* me, you *left* me while—" I didn't finish that sentence, she didn't know about the man who attacked me. Not that she cared to check in or ask during our phone call. James' expression was filled with concern as he watched on helplessly.

"I've never abandoned you," she said sternly.

"You ran away!" My voice was now raised. "I needed you and you ran five hours away, leaving me to fight on my own. You haven't even asked me how I am; you didn't call me to check up on me. Don't pretend any of this was for me when this has always been you doing what is best for you."

"Lucy, that is not—"

"What time did Dad get home that night?" I knew this wasn't how James wanted me to ask this question, but I needed to get off the phone. I couldn't bear to stay on the phone any longer.

"I don't know…" Hesitation filled her voice. "Around midnight, I guess? Why are you asking?" I didn't respond, instead I slammed the phone down. Then I picked it up and slammed it continuously before sobs found their way to the surface. James caught me as I fell down.

James *always* caught me.

141

Twenty-Nine

James

I could hardly stand to watch the phone call; it was difficult not knowing what was said on the other side. Judging by the way Lucy reacted as the call went on, it wasn't good. Her composure slowly slipped and I resisted reaching out. That was until she was off the call and she slumped to the ground in my arms. I had witnessed Lucy cry multiple times since we met and each time was more heartbreaking than the last. I wished I could take her pain away; I was trying, but the process of doing so seemed to hurt her more.

"She lied, James. I know she lied," she said in between sobs.

"Did she say something different to her statement?" Lucy shook her head.

"No, she said the same thing, but she was hesitant. Almost like she had to try to remember what she said." She took a deep breath as she attempted to calm down. "I think you're right. I think she lied out of spite."

James

"Hell hath no fury like a woman scorned." Lucy laughed softly.

"I guess you're right. She kept talking as if there was more to it, though. Like it should have been obvious to me that my father was this monster." I thought back to the uneasy feeling her father gave me, especially the second time meeting him. He had a temper, but then again, most of us had anger inside of us. The difference was some of us had better control of it than others. I hadn't been able to shake the thought that there was more to Anthony than met the eye. I needed to speak to Vera without Lucy in earshot.

"What did she say he's done?"

"She wouldn't say, just insinuating it should be obvious."

"And you can't think of any reason she would say that about your father?" I tried to keep my tone light when asking. I didn't want Lucy to feel like I was pushing her, too.

"Not a single thing," she said with a sigh.

"I'm proud of you for standing up for yourself," I said, planting a kiss on her forehead. I had no interest in pressing her any further, she clearly didn't know anything. She smiled shyly up at me. "Right, come on." I helped her up to her feet. "We are going to head back, give Cato a good walk, and have a nice dinner."

She accepted the help up without complaint and grabbed my hand as we walked back to the car.

"Are you excited to have Daines over?"

"Absolutely, I don't think we've ever been sophisticated enough to have a dinner party. Are you sure you're okay with it? There's still time to cancel."

"Of course I'm okay with it! I'm excited to get Daines to tell me all about what you were like when you were younger.

Especially those teenage years," she teased. Initially, I was excited to have Daines come round, now I was terrified. There was very little that Jack Daines did not know about me.

"As long as he remembers it goes both ways. However bad the stories he tells you are, I've got an arsenal of ones I can tell Angie."

* * *

After we got back, we took some time to relax and eat lunch before going out for a long walk with Cato. Partly to enjoy some fresh air together and partly to wear him out. He was a sweet dog, but he was wild. I'd never met a dog with such high energy. Lucy and I talked more about her father and mother's dynamic when we walked. It was therapeutic to talk about these dark things in beautiful surroundings. She went through every bad thing she could think of about her father, but none of them felt like what her mother was referring to. None of them felt bad enough to warrant him being called a monster.

When we got back, we both started getting ready for the evening. I started to give the place a good clean up when I noticed the record player. There were even some records here. I guess my dad moved this out of the house to here. I put the first record on as I finished cleaning.

"Ooh look at you, setting the ambience," Lucy said mockingly. It took me a while to respond as I was immediately distracted by her appearance. Her hair hung in long, graceful curves over her shoulders. A belt around her dress on her waist accentuated her curves. "Earth to James," she said, a playfulness in her tone as she approached me.

James

"Sorry, you're just..." I shook my head. "Extremely distracting. You look beautiful." I couldn't help but drop my gaze lower as she came close.

"My eyes are up here." Her hand found its way to my chin, tilting it upwards. I flushed slightly at her comment, embarrassed by being caught. "Dance with me?" There was never even a fleeting thought of denying Lucy anything she asked for, even if I was nervous to dance with her. When it came to Lucy Davis, *no* wasn't in my vocabulary.

I took one of her hands in mine and placed my other hand on her waist as we began to sway softly. I allowed myself to relax and the music to influence our movements.

"Can I ask you a question?" Lucy asked after a few minutes of quiet dancing.

"Always."

"What's the deal with what's going on between us? What are we doing?" The forwardness of the question should have surprised me, but it didn't. Lucy always seemed to be good at communicating her thoughts with me.

"You mean this?" I asked, spinning her round. "Just an entirely normal lawyer-client relationship." She met my words with a hearty laugh.

"I'm being serious, James!" she said, struggling to contain her laughter.

"I'm not sure what exactly it is, but I do know I'm enjoying it and I want it to continue," I answered honestly.

"I like that answer."

"Thank you, I thought of it myself." She hit my side playfully. "I know you have a lot going on, Lucy. I don't want you to feel overwhelmed or pressured into anything. I want to be a support to you, not a burden."

"You've never once made me feel pressured." Relief flooded through me at her words. "You are right, there is a lot happening in my life." I don't know why I felt nervous, this was exactly why I hadn't brought it up. I didn't want Lucy to feel backed into a corner. "But I don't want it to stand in the way of something good. I don't want the situation to push you away from me."

"I went into this knowing that the case has to come first, I'm not going to be pushed away by it. I'm here, Lucy." I brought her hand to her chest. "I am right here and I will still be here when this is all over. We don't have to rush anything; we have all the time in the world."

"Thank you, I don't think I would be able to cope with all this without you."

"Of course, you would; you're Lucy Davis. You're the bravest person I know. Although, don't say I said that in front of Daines, he's a bit sensitive."

She threw her head back with a laugh. "You're a pretty good dancer, Weatherston."

"You just wait until some hip hop comes on, that's when my real moves will come out."

"Oh, I would pay good money to see that."

"Besides, dancing gives me an excuse to be close to you." She leant her head into my chest as we swayed.

Thirty

Lucy

I could have quite happily danced in James' arms for the rest of the night, but it was only an hour till our guests arrived and I had food to prep. I considered myself a good cook, but I had never hosted a dinner party before and I was nervous. It was so much more than just the food, there was the social element to it, too. These were important people to James and James was important to me. I wanted Daines to like me. As far as I was aware, he didn't know about anything romantic happening between us two since this is a recent development. Would he tell James it was a bad idea?

My feelings for James seemed to get stronger every day, but it didn't change the circumstances of how we met. It didn't change the off-balanced dynamic between the two of us. Whilst he may be working the case for free, the power balance is off. He's been hired to work a case by me. Those who were not a part of this or hadn't seen how we progressed may judge us. I wouldn't blame Daines if he wasn't keen. I wouldn't blame him for being protective over his friend.

"Need any help, boss?" As sweet as it was, James' nickname only seemed to heighten my worry about this.

"No, I'm all good food wise. Maybe just get the drinks all ready?" Hosting a dinner party together was a very couple thing to do for two people who weren't putting a label on their relationship. Despite the cabin being rundown, it was starting to feel like a home. It was James and I's safe place where we could just be together without judgement.

A loud knock on the door made me jump and I watched James cross the room to answer it. Daines embraced James as he crossed the threshold before turning to introduce Angie. She was a tall brunette woman with piercing blue eyes. I could see why Daines was so taken with her; the two seemed to comfortably fall in step with each other. I wondered if James and I looked as well matched next to each other.

"Lucy-Lou." Daines approached me like he had known me for years before pulling me into a hug. "These are for you." He grabbed a bunch of flowers from Angie so she could hug me before giving them to me.

"You didn't have to do that," I said as I took them in my hands.

"You've had to put up being in this cabin with James for a few days, you deserve them." His eyes met James as James rolled his eyes at him. James immediately engaged with Angie as he poured some wine for everyone. Asking her about what she does for a living and generic family questions. James seemed to be a natural conversationalist; people seemed to just be comfortable talking to him. I couldn't help but smile as I watched the interaction. Daines caught my eye briefly

Lucy

and smiled before turning his attention back to them. He was clearly enjoying the interaction like I was.

As we sat at the table, the topic of conversation turned to me.

"Do you have a plan yet of how long you're going to stay in town?" Daines directed the question to both of us, but looked at me.

"I'm not really sure, a few more days, maybe?" I looked quizzingly at James.

"I would think until we are done with the case or the trial starts." The idea of a trial made me feel sick, watching my father on the stands. I couldn't bear it.

"How is that all going?" Daines asked hesitantly. Angie didn't look confused, so I imagine he's already filled her in on who I am. I appreciated that neither of them treated me differently.

"Well, I was going to ask for your help," James said, earning a raised brow from Daines.

"Help with the case?" he questioned. James nodded.

"I didn't want to talk about it over dinner, but I was hoping to use your police officer brain on a couple things later on, if that's okay?" Daines looked lost in thought for a moment before answering.

"On one condition." A wave of nausea hit me. "If I'm going to help you solve this mystery, I'm Fred and you're Shaggy."

"Why the fuck do I have to be Shaggy?" Angie and I both broke out in laughter, the seriousness in James' tone sending me over the edge. He seemingly was deeply offended by being likened to Shaggy.

"What, you want to be the fucking dog? He's Scooby." Daines pointed to Cato asleep on the couch. James sat back in a huff with his arms crossed and I had to put a hand on my chest because I was laughing so hard.

"Are you guys seriously arguing about hypothetically which *Scooby-Doo* characters you would be?" Angie asked in between laughs. James' gaze fell on me and I saw a rose tint in his cheeks, clearly embarrassed with how offended he had gotten. He took a deep breath before speaking.

"Hey, Angie, do you want to hear what happened when Daines asked Clara to a school dance?"

"Don't you dare." The colour in Daines' cheeks now matched James.

"He was *convinced* she was desperately in love with him," James began, his eyes staring straight at Daines as he spoke. "Have you ever heard Daines sing?" Angie shook her head. "You're a lucky lady, it's like a cat being dragged kicking and screaming through a hedge."

Now it was Daines' turn to sulk as he sat back in his chair.

"Clara loved classic rock, and lover boy over here," he pointed to Daines with a smirk, "thought he should write her a song to ask her to prom. My stupid self agreed to give him a drum beat whilst the other Jack played the guitar." James paused to let out a small laugh at the memory. "When I tell you this girl begged him to stop, she literally *begged* him. I did feel awful for you at the time, Daines, but since I have lost my sympathy, it was clear she was in love with this guy, Ashton. Who she is now married to, by the way."

"What can I say, baby?" Daines said, turning to Angie. "I'm just a hopeless romantic." He kissed her and James made a retching sound. "Anyway, like you can talk, Weatherston. You asked three girls to the dance that year and every single one said no."

Lucy

"I had a broken fucking leg, of course they said no. Nobody wants to go to a dance with a guy who can't stand up to dance."

"Oh my God, that is so sad!" I said, placing my hand on James instinctively. I realised right after that I probably shouldn't have; he hadn't told Daines yet about us. I had no idea if he even wanted Daines to know something was going on between us. James brought my hand up to his mouth and kissed it softly.

"None of that really matters now," he said with a shrug.

Thirty-One

James

I don't know why I was so nervous about Daines and Lucy interacting, I was just desperate for them to get on. They were the two most important people in my life and I wanted us to be able to all get together like this.

They got on like a house on fire and I couldn't care less that it was at my expense. Daines could tell embarrassing stories about me all night if it made Lucy smile like that. We finished up our mains and had a brief respite before dessert.

"Fancy a cigar?" Daines nodded his head towards the door.

"Sure, back in a sec." I touched Lucy lightly on the shoulder before heading out to the porch.

"So, when did you and Lucy become a thing? Before or after you took her case?" he asked as he lit my cigar.

"We aren't really a—"

"Don't even start, Weatherston. You have literal hearts in your eyes when you look at her."

James

"Nothing happened until after we saw you at the store."

"When did you start to like her?"

"About two seconds after I saw her for the first time." He laughed softly.

"I knew you were gone bad, but I didn't know you were *that* gone." He took a drag of his cigar. "Why are you working the case here? What made you come home?"

I was dreading telling him this, but if I wanted his help he needed the full story. "Lucy was attacked." His eyes widened. "She was out walking Cato by her home and a man tried to kill her, strangled her in some kind of sick attempt for justice for Amber."

"Fuck…" Daines said, taking another drag of his cigar. "Was he arrested?" I shook my head. "Is that why you want my help on the case?"

"Partly, I need your help finding out who he was and making sure he sees justice."

"And the other part?"

"Do you have connections with Kirkston City PD?" He nodded. "I want to find out more about Lucy's mother, Vera. Do you think you could ask them if they met her and if she said anything of interest whilst she was there making her statement?"

"Yeah, I'll give them a call on Monday, see what I can find out." I was grateful for Daines' unwavering support. It didn't matter if he thought I was making the stupidest decision, he was always there.

"Thank you, I really appreciate it."

"Anything for you, James, you know that." He patted my shoulder. "I told you that you could do both, didn't I?"

"Do both?"

"Get the girl and build the career at the same time." I sighed; he didn't know about what happened with Michael, either. I'd been holding it close to my chest.

"I got fired." His head snapped round immediately. "Well, I haven't *officially* been fired yet. Michael said if I didn't come back by Monday I was fired." He looked at me for a moment, I very rarely left him speechless. The impending ultimatum Michael had left me had been nagging at me.

"Lucy doesn't know, does she?" I shook my head. "Are you going to go back by Monday?"

"No." The words felt so final, I don't think I'd ever even thought about going back. "I can't guarantee Lucy's safety until we catch the guy who attacked her. Even then she will have reporters swarming all over her, we need to stay here until it's all over with."

"That's a big decision, James. Are you sure you're okay giving it up? You are always going on about how important your career is to you."

"I've never been more sure of anything in my entire life." We both sat back in our chairs, looking out over the lake. My words were heavy, but saying them out loud made me feel lighter. I had been going round and round in my head about what to do. This whole time, however, I knew in my heart Lucy was my first choice. Michael could shove his job where the sun didn't shine. I would choose her every single time.

"Angie is pretty amazing," I said after a while.

"She's really something, isn't she?"

"You talked about me being gone, but you're just as gone as I am." He laughed loudly.

"We are just a couple of suckers in love, aren't we?" He took a swig from his glass.

James

"Cheers to that." I clinked my glass against his before taking another sip and putting it down next to me. "I'm glad you're happy, Daines. Really, I am pleased for you."

"And you, buddy. All I ever want is for you to be happy." His words made me smile and I was glad Lucy had suggested this dinner. "And I'm really glad to have you home, even if it's only for a few days. Will you promise to visit more?"

"It's been really good being here. I don't know what the future holds, but I have a feeling we may be staying put after this."

"Really?" Daines sat back up, excitement in his voice.

"I don't want to get your hopes up, but Lucy and I spoke about it briefly. We both feel like this is where we are supposed to be. I guess it all just depends on how everything goes."

"I am literally crossing every damn part of my body for that to happen." He was animated as he spoke. "Can you imagine it, James? We're both married, living in Rosehaven. We have some kids and teach each other's kids bad words. Then we are growing old, drinking beer on the porch and reminiscing about old times." His words prompted a laugh from me. "That's the fucking dream right there."

"Alright, Daines, don't get yourself all excited. Nothing is set in stone. I reckon we should focus on getting through this dinner first."

"I guess you're right. We should probably get inside. There are two beautiful women waiting for us in there."

"And a pumpkin pie," I said, putting out my cigar.

"And a pumpkin pie." He laughed, putting out his own before heading back inside.

Thirty-Two

Lucy

"Do you mind if I ask how you are doing with everything?" Angie asked, pouring us both another glass once the boys were outside. "We don't have to talk about it if you don't want to."

I liked Angie; she seemed sweet and had a good sense of humour. You had to have that if you were around either Daines or James—those two were constantly cracking jokes. If I did end up staying in Rosehaven, I hoped the two of us would become friends.

"I don't mind. It's been hard, but James has really helped a lot."

"He seems like a good guy. D talks about him all the time, I think he's missed having him around."

"James is the same, it's a shame they haven't been able to see each other a lot."

"They talk on the phone a lot; James scared him the other

Lucy

night calling so late. I think he just wanted someone to speak to." My chest twinged thinking about it. James never really spoke about anyone else but Daines to me regarding friends. I know he has a strained relationship with his family, so it must have been quite lonely in the city. Before all of this, I had a friend group which I thought were everything. We always chatted about life with each other and I felt included. Since my father's arrest, I have felt so lonely. Was this how James felt all the time? Loneliness was the hardest thing I had ever been through, feeling like you had nowhere to turn. It weighed heavy on my soul.

"I think we need to make sure the two of them see each other a bit more."

"Agreed," Angie said with a smile. "They are both very lucky to have us, eh?" I laughed as the door opened and they walked back in.

"Ready for dessert?" I asked, looking over to them.

"I'm on it," James said as he walked past me, stopping to kiss the top of my head. He seemed to have a spring in his step as he bounced towards the kitchen. Reconnecting with Daines and his home clearly did him good.

"You have him well trained already," Daines joked as he sat back down. We talked more over dessert about pretty much everything and anything. I listened intently when they told stories about things they got up to around town. I imagined a younger James, a James before the crash growing up with his sister. I thought about how the weight of survivor's guilt weighed him down now. Whilst fundamentally I know he is similar, there are aspects of him now that are different from his younger version I hear stories of. The version of James now carries around a pain inside him, a silent struggle.

Till Death Parts Us

After finishing the pie, I got up and started taking the dishes to the sink.

"Let me help," Daines said, hopping out of his seat and following me into the kitchen area "I'll wash, you dry?" I grabbed a tea towel and he started filling the sink.

"Thank you for coming tonight, James seems really happy to have you here," I said, lowering my voice so James couldn't hear across the room.

"I don't think I'm the one responsible for his happiness," he said with a smirk as he began washing. "I think most of that is because of you." I blushed slightly at his words.

"He's a good guy, I'm grateful that he is helping me with all of this."

"James never does something unless he really wants to. He took your case because it meant something to him, because *you* mean something to him." He passed me over a plate to dry. "James says you have been enjoying being here in Rosehaven?"

"Truthfully, it's starting to feel like home. The home I once knew is gone now and I feel safe here." Our eyes met briefly as he passed me another plate. I didn't know how much James had told him outside.

"You *are* safe here."

"Thank you for offering to help on the case as well. I don't know what James has asked of you, but any time you can spare I'm grateful for."

"Of course, I'd do anything for James, and by extension, I will do anything for you, too. Welcome to our weird little family, Lucy-Lou." I laughed as I dried up the last of the dishes. After everything was cleared away, we said our goodbyes and made promises to do it again. I meant that promise, I wanted this to be part of my new normal. The new life I was building.

Lucy

"Well, that was a good night," James said as we cuddled together on the sofa. "I am definitely going to gain some serious weight dating you," he teased. "You know how to cook a good meal."

"I better be careful, I'll end up spoiling you."

"Sweetheart, you've already spoiled me." He turned my face towards him and kissed me.

"Maybe I need to dial back some privileges," I said against his lips.

"Please don't." There was a slight beg to his voice and his lips recaptured mine, more demanding than they were before. There was an urgency in the way he kissed me, like he was always worried it would be the last chance. I matched his urgency, giving myself freely to him as I made my way onto his lap.

His lips made the journey from my lips down to my neck and my shoulders. His hands hesitated on the back of my dress as our eyes met.

"Sorry," he said softly. "I didn't mean to get carried away."

"James…" I lifted his chin with my hand. "I *want* you to get carried away." He looked at me. It was clear he knew this was permission, but he still seemed nervous.

"I need you to promise me this is okay, Lucy. I need you to promise me this is what you want."

"I *promise* this is exactly what I want." He smiled and I watched the nervousness leave his expression.

"Perfect." He kissed me again. "But not with this damn dog watching us," he said as he gestured towards Cato. I laughed as James flung me over his shoulders, carrying me towards the bedroom and slamming the door shut behind us.

Thirty-Three

James

Michael had asked me if I was following my mind or my dick when I made the decision to take Lucy to Rosehaven. The truth was neither of them, although they both reaped the rewards. It was my heart that took the lead when it came to her. As we lay in bed with her sleeping softly beside me, I know that given the choice, I would do it all again. I had no regrets in what I had done. For so many years, I had unknowingly let my fear and anxieties lead me.

I had always wanted to gain justice for those who deserved it, but it was my parents' pushing that really put me on the track to become a lawyer. They wanted me to become something great to account for everything they had lost. I wondered if without their pushing, would I have become an officer with Daines? Would we be partners out working shifts together? It was a nice thought, but I don't regret the path I've got. No,

James

I'm happy being a lawyer.

What I am not happy with is finding that justice on other people's terms. Only taking cases that someone else tells me are worth it. I want to help more people like Lucy, people that everyone else shut down without taking the time to really listen to what is in front of them. These firms focus on statistics and easy wins rather than the people behind the crimes. I had dreamed of being a lawyer like Michael Sawyer, but now I want to be the complete opposite of him. I wanted to fight for all people, to put the time and energy in anybody that asked. I would make sure not just the person on trial, but the families behind them had support they needed. A case was so much more than just a person on trial, than just a statistic.

I didn't care if I never became rich or was considered successful. I didn't care if my decisions would disappoint my parents. Lucy was right; I needed to live, and live in the way that I wanted to, not in the shadow of what others want me to.

Lucy let out a groan beside me as her eyes opened.

"Morning, sunshine," I teased, brushing a hand through her hair. She sat up, prompting me to pull myself up next to her.

"Morning." Her voice was still half asleep as she leant her head on me.

"How are you feeling?" There was a small part of me that was worried she would regret last night, regret giving me permission. The last thing I ever want is for her to feel obligated or pressured by me.

"Pretty amazing." She turned her head to smirk up at me and I allowed a smile to creep onto my face. "For the first time in a week, I actually feel like a normal person."

"Are you sure you want to ruin that by going to see my

parents today?" I shuddered inwardly at the thought. "We could just stay in bed all day instead."

"You can't hide from them forever." She rolled her eyes. "You'll have me there. If in doubt, you can just talk about what a mess my life is to make them feel better about yours."

"Lucy!" I tickled her playfully.

"I'm only messing," she said with a laugh. "Come on, let's get up and get ready for this."

* * *

I was quiet on the drive to my parents' house; I could feel the nerves bubbling away in my chest. It has been a year since I had seen them in person and weeks since we'd spoken on the phone. They still lived in the house we grew up in, so reminders of Alice were everywhere. It was an emotionally taxing experience, but I was grateful to have Lucy here for support. When we pulled up outside, I felt frozen in place.

"Are you ready?" Lucy asked tentatively. I don't think I would ever be ready for this.

"How would you feel if I introduced you as my girlfriend?" The question had been on my tongue all morning, but I hadn't felt brave enough to ask. Lucy's eyes widened. "It's just I would introduce you as my friend, but I feel like it lessens what you are to me."

"Are you sure? Given our connection and my father, I wouldn't mind if we toned it down. I know this is hard enough for you as it is." *She wasn't saying no, she didn't say no.*

"I'm sure. I have no interest in hiding how I feel for you. You're important to me and I want them to know that."

James

"Then I would be happy for you to introduce me that way," she said, gripping my hand. "But if you change your mind when that door opens, I won't be angry with you."

What did I do to deserve her?

I took a deep breath before opening the car door. I hadn't bothered to call ahead, but both of their cars were in the drive. They usually had quiet days on Sundays, so I knew they'd be here. Lucy took her place by my side as we walked up to the door. My hand shook as I rang the bell.

My mother was the one to open the door, her eyes widening in shock. She looked frailer than I remembered. You forget as you grow up your parents are growing old.

"Hey, Ma." A nervous smile gracing my lips.

"James!" She embraced me tightly in a way that felt unexpected to me. As she moved away, her eyes caught Lucy's.

"This is *my girlfriend,* Lucy." The words came out effortlessly and I felt a sense of pride as I spoke. The two embraced and then my mother ushered us inside.

"Did you drive here this morning?" Her voice was uncharacteristically happy.

"Actually, we've been staying in the cabin since Thursday," I replied awkwardly. "Sorry, I meant to call ahead, but I didn't really have the time."

"Oh, don't worry about that, your father never uses it. Where is he, anyway?" She moved to the stairs. "Eric?" she called up the stairs. I heard his footsteps stomping down. His eyes briefly looked at me before they fell on Lucy. His face dropped when he looked at her, the colour draining from it.

The way his eyes were trained on her made me feel uneasy as the tension in the room heightened.

Thirty-Four

Lucy

You could cut the atmosphere in the room with a knife. James' father, Eric, seemed frozen in place when he came down the stairs.

"I've seen you before." His hand pointed towards me and I suddenly felt sick.

"This is James' girlfriend, Lucy," James' mother said.

"Lucy *Davis*," he emphasised my last name in a way that made my skin crawl. "I saw a picture of you in the paper."

My stomach dropped. *He'd read about my father.* I saw a photo of me outside my home that made the paper yesterday. James had tried to throw it out before I read it, but I saw it in the bin. It wasn't the clearest picture, but I guess if you saw me the next day you'd remember it.

"Your father, he *killed* someone." My head spun as I leant against the wall for support. I knew they would find out who I was, but this was not how I expected this to start.

Lucy

"*Allegedly.*" A sharpness took hold of James' tone as he addressed his father. "It's nice to see you, too, Dad."

"Why don't I make us some coffee?" His mother's voice came out squeaky.

"Good idea, Mags," his dad said, brushing past us and heading to the living room. James turned to me, offering his arm for support. He mouthed *I'm sorry* as we followed his father through. There was silence for a while as we waited for his mom to make drinks and make her own way into the room. I clutched that coffee in my hand like a comfort blanket, taking a sip whilst I tried to ignore the awkwardness in the air. I can see why James didn't want to be here.

"I'm working the Anthony Davis case," James spoke first.

"Michael took it on?" His Dad looked at him quizzingly. "That surprises me, he always seems quite picky from what you've told me." If I wasn't already feeling sick before, my entire breakfast was going to come out now. James had told me that he always felt like he was disappointing his parents, taking the case outside of work wasn't going to help matters.

"No." James shook his head. "I am working on it on my own. It'll be my first solo case."

"Oh, James, that's great!" His mother beamed, but his father raised his hand.

"And Michael was okay with that? You're wasting time on this case." His words were another punch to my chest. He's like so many others who had written my father off.

"I actually don't work for Michael anymore. Well, I won't work for him from Monday onwards." My gaze shot to James; this was new information to me. I could tell he was avoiding my eyes as he looked straight on at his mother, clearly trying to avoid his father's gaze, too.

"Why not? You had a good opportunity there. Don't throw it away."

"He said if I stayed here and worked Anthony's case, then I was fired. I am staying and I am working the case." He grabbed my hand, still avoiding my eyes.

"Don't be fucking stupid, James." His father slammed his empty cup down. "You're going to throw it away for…" He waved his hands, gesturing towards me.

"For me?" My voice dripped with sarcasm.

"Yes, for you. Do you know how hard he has worked? What lies did you spin to convince him to throw his career away, eh?" He turned to look at James. "You realise if her father is a murderer, she's probably crazy in this head as well?"

"Enough!" James shouted, causing me to jump as his mother let out a gasp. "Do you want me to walk out that door?"

"No, of course not," Mags' desperate voice broke out. His father paused before he shook his head.

"If you ever talk to her like that again, I will walk out that door and you will never see me again. Do you understand?" They both nodded their heads, his father leaning back in his chair. I didn't know where to look. I felt like I should speak, but no words came to the surface.

"Anthony did not kill Amber." His father started to speak, but he held his hand up. "Don't you question me. It is not because of what I have been told. I saw him with my own eyes, I spoke to him twice. I questioned that man myself. *He did not do it.*" James has often said he agreed with me about my father's innocence. I wondered before if he said it to appease me, because he cared about me. Listening to him saying it now, he truly believed it, too. These were not just words.

"I was miserable working at Michael's firm, *fucking miserable.*

Lucy

Nobody there cared if I lived or died, and I was starting to not care if I lived or died either." His voice broke at the last word. "I went to work, sat behind my desk all day, and just stared at files. I would call people, reject their cases, and have to listen to them beg me to take on their cases or their families' cases." His eyes looked at me now, tears forming in them as he did. "Then I would go home to my apartment on my own and spend my evening looking through case files and eating frozen meals for one. All night I would think about those families who begged me for help. They needed help and we shot them down without even really looking into anything."

"James, why didn't you ever say anything?" His mother looked between him and his father.

"All you two ever care about is my work, how successful I am or how I'm going to progress my career. You never cared about me."

"Of course we cared about you," his father interjected.

"Not once did you ask me about anything other than my work. Not once." My heart was breaking for him, I squeezed his hand. This was his time to say what he needed to and I was by his side as he did.

"It was never our intention to make you feel that way." Eric's voice had softened significantly as he looked down at his hands. I watched James' gaze move to the pictures on the wall. One included him standing next to a girl, who I assumed to be Alice. They looked almost identical except her hair was lighter.

"I'm not Alice," he said suddenly. "I will never be Alice."

"We know that," Mags said, her voice shocked.

"Do you? Sometimes I feel like you wished I had died instead of her." He seemed to no longer be able to hold his tears in as they rolled down his cheeks. I removed my hand from his and grabbed hold of his arm. "I don't feel like I'll ever be good enough for you, that nothing I do is good enough because I'm not her."

His father didn't look up, but tears mimicking James' rolled down his mother's cheeks.

"James, that's not true." She nudged her husband.

"We weren't trying to compare the two of you. It's just..." His father paused. "...hard that you are now older than she ever got to be. You are all we have left. It's not that we wanted you to feel pressured, we just wanted you to get the most out of life."

"You know, it was *Lucy* who told me I needed to start living," James said, turning his attention to me. "For the longest time, I was just in survival mode—trying to be everything else everyone wanted me to be. Lucy showed me that I needed to start being who I wanted to be." I didn't particularly want to cry in front of his parents, but James was making it extremely difficult.

His father paused for a moment before looking me in the eye. "I'm sorry, Lucy, I didn't mean to be so abrupt," his father said, offering me an apologetic smile. I felt the tension start to lessen in the room. It wasn't perfect, but this was a start.

Thirty-Five

James

Without Lucy by my side, I don't know how I would have faced this conversation. With her, I felt stronger than I had ever been. I had no intentions of coming here for a confrontation, but listening to the way my father spoke down to Lucy made me see red. Once that can of worms was open, there was no way I could stop it.

I said things that I had never done out loud before. It wasn't until this moment I realised quite how close to the edge I had been. I was miserable in my life in Kirkston City. I hadn't been happy since I left for college, that was the truth of it. I went to college and studied day and night to get my law degree. Sure, there were people I was friendly with, parties and a few girls here and there, but none of it made me happy. None of it filled the void I had in me.

"It's okay, I know my situation is a little unique," Lucy said, responding to my father's apology. "It looks bad, but I really believe he didn't do it." I was grateful the conversation was shifting focus away from me.

"How is the case going?" My father's eyes darted between the two of us.

"It's complicated. I'm worried about going to trial, I'm trying to do everything to prevent it." I noticed all eyes looking at me quizzingly. "A trial will likely last a long time, especially a murder trial. They will also go into detail about every little part of the family's lives, you included, Lucy." I let out a sigh. "We just need to find something either concrete that says he didn't or concrete that says someone else did."

"I imagine you didn't come here to talk about the case, why don't the two of you stay for lunch? Maybe we can talk about things other than work," my mother said. I was grateful that she was at least trying to take in what I had said. I wasn't sure if Lucy wanted to stay, but she quickly jumped in.

"We'd love to. I bet there are tons of stories you can tell me about James," she said teasingly as she beamed up at me.

The lunch went better than I had expected, although I felt anxious to get back to work. As much as I enjoyed this time, there was something big looming over us and I was running out of time. I meant what I said—I couldn't let this go to trial. Anthony would not represent well; the prosecution would push him and push him until he broke. If he even showed a fraction of the anger he did to me on the stand, he would be finished. A jury would immediately see him as guilty; they would think Amber said something he didn't like and he snapped. I wouldn't be able to save him if he lost his temper.

Then there was Lucy; it was highly likely she would be called up to the stand as a character witness, if nothing else. They would grill her over everything. They would want to know

James

if there were signs, they would make her feel like she missed important details. I don't know if I could watch her go through that, but I wouldn't have a choice. If this went to trial, I would have to watch them tear her entire family's lives apart and there would be nothing I could do.

There was outside of the trial, too. The number of reporters would be even worse. They would find out where she was and camp outside until it was all over. Any glimpse of a life or fun would be gone for her. I needed to either prove he was innocent or that someone else is guilty, and I needed to do it in the next few days. Anthony was going to be given his date within the next week or so, I couldn't let it get that far.

"What are you thinking about?" Lucy asked as we walked back to my car.

"The case."

"Me too," she said solemnly. "I can't stop thinking that we aren't going to find out what happened and they are just going to make him guilty for an easy win."

"I promise you, Lucy, that isn't what is going to happen. Your father won't have to sit in that cell for much longer."

"You can't promise that, James."

"Yes, I can. I know you haven't known me very long, but when I make a promise I keep it. Trust me, Lucy, I've got this." I held my voice strong even though I didn't feel it inside. I knew I was playing a dangerous game making promises like these, but I couldn't help it. I wasn't going to watch Lucy suffer through a trial and truthfully, I wasn't sure I trusted my skill set in a trial yet, either. I was still a rookie compared to most of the other lawyers working in the city. They would probably eat me alive in the courtroom with this case .

I would do anything I could to get Anthony free, even if it

meant going against everything I had believed until this point. I wouldn't sleep again until he was free, if that was what it took.

Anthony Davis would not go down for Amber Jones' murder.

Thirty-Six

Lucy

There was something about James' promise that made me feel uneasy.

Not in a way I thought he would do anything untoward, just that I felt like he would keep going with this case even if it completely burnt him out. His expression had a determination that I hadn't ever seen before. I think he was even more desperate to free my father than I was. For him, he had the pressure of both his career being on the line and his care for me. I hadn't really even thought about a trial until he brought it up with his parents. I know that was naïve of me, but I had really thought we'd find something and it would be easy. I should have realised none of this was going to be easy.

When we got back to the cabin, James immediately started going through his case files and I knew he was locked into the activity. I couldn't help but have some worry in the back of my mind about him. We positioned ourselves in the bedroom so we could spread everything out and go through it bit by bit.

"Do you think the sleeping pills aspect is a little odd?" The question had been on my mind for days, but with everything else going I had forgotten to discuss it with James.

"What do you mean?"

"You've met my dad, he's a big guy. It would have been absolutely nothing for him to overpower Amber, so why use the pills?"

"Because he was scared?" James asked questioningly before pulling a face.

"What?"

"Your dad doesn't strike me a man who would be scared," he followed up, clearly disagreeing with his own question. "So, you think whoever did it was smaller?"

"Smaller or not confident in what they were doing." As much as I didn't believe my father did it, I think if he had, he wouldn't have used this method.

"It's definitely a lead worth following. Maybe we can see if Amber had an ex or another boyfriend or something."

"Jealousy is definitely a motive."

"It may be worth speaking to your dad again, see if maybe the killer was a woman. If we are considering jealousy as a motive, we need to consider both angles."

"My mother?" I felt like James was trying to beat around the bush and it was grating on me. "There is no way she is involved in this."

"I'm not saying she is. Your father could have been seeing other women. We need to keep an open mind with all this and not write off options because they hurt."

He was right, of course he was right. My mother had to be

added to the list of suspects, regardless of how it made me feel. We had to explore every single option that was available to us and start crossing them off bit by bit.

"What about me?" He raised his eyebrow in response. "You said we need to keep an open mind on this, my name should be on there."

"You didn't kill Amber," he said firmly.

"We shouldn't write off options just because they hurt," I said, mimicking his previous phrase. If we were going to be open minded, my name needed to be on there. I watched him hesitatingly write my name down.

"What about the man that attacked you? He should be on the list." I shook my head.

"He should be crossed off. Attacking me was him getting revenge *for* Amber, it wouldn't make sense that he also killed her. Besides, we don't even know who he is."

"We don't know who he is *yet*."

"We are not trying to find out who he is, we are trying to find out who killed Amber."

"Why can't I do both?" he said sternly. "This man attacked you, Lucy. He can't just get away with it." His voice raised slightly. "He clearly has some connection to Amber. It wouldn't be hard to track him down, to make him pay."

"James, please," I said, my voice begging. "I just want to focus on finding Amber's killer, everything else can wait." He was quiet for a moment as I watched him taking deep breaths. The stress of it all was clearly getting to him. As I looked at our list of suspects, I couldn't help but feel slightly overwhelmed, as well. There were a lot of options and not a lot of answers.

"Okay, but as soon as we find Amber's killer, I am going after him next." I wasn't going to argue with James, I could see it wouldn't do any good. He was a kind man, but he also had this stubbornness about him. When he set his mind to something, convincing him off it was impossible.

"So, where should we start?"

"There are a few character witnesses from Amber's friends, some knew of your father and some didn't. I think we need to go through them critically. Any that strike us as odd, we should set up a meeting with them." I nodded and got to work.

Every so often I looked at James, his hair all over the place as he kept playing with it. Kept shuffling it about. The stress was evident on his face. My worries were continuing to grow each minute.

I was worried about James, about how this was all affecting him. He'd lost his job for the case; I can't imagine the pressure he had building inside of him. It had only also been hours since he confronted his parents about emotions he had been holding in for years. I tried to debrief with him in the car, but he wasn't interested in speaking about it. His mind was completely on my father's case.

I was also worried about my father. Every so often, flashes of him in prison crossed my mind. It broke my heart to think of him being in there. As more time went on, the more worried I was that we would fail. That we would fail and he would spend the rest of his life in prison for something he didn't do.

Thirty-Seven

James

"We're going out," Lucy exclaimed, throwing the papers in a heap on the bed.

"We have work to do," I reminded her, lowering my own stack of papers. I felt like I had read these words over and over, but no solution was jumping out at me.

"We *need* to take a break. I don't know about you, but my brain is fried." She was right, of course. Lucy always was. Not in an overly confident way, she was just incredibly observant. She always seemed to know how everybody else around her was feeling.

"Let's go dancing!" She jumped up excitedly. My eyes widened as they met hers.

"Dancing?" I asked as she made her way over to me, her feet bouncing with each movement. I wished I could take a picture of this moment. The way her messy hair hung on her shoulders, the sunset hitting her just right, making her glow.

Till Death Parts Us

The way she smiled when she looked at me. Her beauty was effortless. She was *flawless*.

I didn't know what the future held for me, but I knew I needed Lucy Davis to be a part of it.

"Yes, *James*, let's go down to Pegasus Bar that your friend Daines was talking about at dinner." Her hands found their way into mine and I gripped onto them. "You must have been there before?"

I shook my head. "I can't say my life has had a lot of time for dancing in it."

"Well, it's about time you started making space in your life for dancing," she said as she removed her hands from mine and placed them on my shoulders.

"Yes, boss," I said, giving a mock salute which was met with an eye roll. My hands gravitated to her hips as I pulled her closer.

"I need to go get ready; I hope I've packed something good enough to wear out. I did it all in such a rush."

"Baby, you could wear a trash bag and you'd still be the prettiest girl in the room."

"Behave, Weatherston." *Never.*

She hit me playfully, laughing as she walked away. I watched her for a moment as she started going through her suitcase. Everything was tossed to the side until she finally settled on a red dress, holding it up to her body and turning round to show me.

"What do you think?" she asked shyly.

"Perfect," I reassured her. She smiled and walked towards the bathroom. I got up and went towards my own clothes. Usually, I wasn't too worried about what I was wearing, but it was different now. I needed to find something to wear that made me look good enough to be standing by Lucy's side. I'm not sure an outfit like that existed. I don't know if I'd ever feel like I deserved her. I wanted things between us to be more official than just a title, but I was scared. Scared to break this bubble we had built in the cabin. Scared she would realise I wasn't good enough for her. Scared she would see the real me, a broken boy who was desperate to be loved without having to ask. The boy who always felt like he was the second choice, the one his parents were left with rather than wanted.

I didn't want her to have this boy version of me. I wanted her to have me as a man. A man who would stand by her side no matter what, who would fight in her corner, always. A man who was strong, confident, and brave. I wanted to be the man who would stop at nothing to give Lucy whatever she wanted.

I felt like I could be that man, I could do that for her. If she would let me.

Once I was ready, I heard the bathroom door open and swung round to see her. A wide smile graced my lips as I took her in. Every single inch of her was perfect.

God, I hoped she let me be that man for her.

Before she spoke, I moved across the room to her, grabbing by the hand and spinning her around.

"You take my breath away, you know that?" I asked as I pulled her towards me, her lips finding mine as we embraced. I moved away to take her in again. I almost didn't want to go out, I didn't want to share her with anyone else. I didn't want other men seeing her and thinking they had a chance with her. They didn't. *She was mine*. As we made our way out of the cabin, I kept my hand linked with hers, even as we drove into town, my hand was on her leg. I was desperate to be close to her. We hadn't talked about the case once since we left. I think we both needed a break from thinking about it. Instead, we talked about the future and all the things we wanted to do. I pulled up just down the street from the bar.

"Do you think you're going to be some fancy lawyer in the city some day?" she asked.

"I used to think that."

"And now?"

"Now I'm not so sure," I answered. "My priorities have shifted since then," I said, turning to look at her.

"What do you mean?" she asked softly.

"I used to think that my career was going to be the most important thing in my life, I was wrong. I know now it won't ever come close to what actually is the most important thing."

"And what's that?"

"*You.*"

I heard her breath hitch as I spoke and silence briefly filled the car before I continued.

"I love you, Lucy."

"You love me?" I felt her hand fall on top of mine and I pulled her hand to my chest.

"With every bit of my soul." Her eyes found mine and I could see tears forming in the side of it.

"I love you, too." Her voice was soft, but there was no shake to it. She meant what she said. I felt the car spin as I moved quickly towards her, pushing my lips against hers. I felt like I was a man starved as the kiss deepened. Lucy was the only one who could fulfil this hunger. Several moments passed before we pulled apart and she looked at me with a wide smile.

"Are you ready to dance with me, Weatherston?" she teased.

"I will always be ready to dance with you, boss." She laughed as she got out of my car and we headed into Pegasus together.

Thirty-Eight

Lucy

It had only been minutes since James had told me he loved me and I was desperate to hear him say it again. He was intoxicating and I needed every last drop of him. I needed to hear him tell me he loves me for the rest of my life. The feeling had been bubbling away inside of me for days, but until I heard him say it, I hadn't quite realised it myself.

I loved James Weatherston and he loved me.

I stayed close to his side as we walked into the bar. Officially, I wasn't actually old enough yet to be in a bar, still a few months off my twenty-first birthday, but nobody questioned me. I was surprised that it was so busy on a Sunday night; part of me had hoped we'd have the dance floor to ourselves. Without hesitation, James held my hand, walking me across to get a drink. James was a gentleman through and through and I knew with him I'd want for nothing.

I walked ahead of him slightly and it was only as I reached a nearby table when I realised James was no longer behind me. I panicked briefly before I noticed that he had been caught by someone for a conversation. From the way they were talking, I could tell he knew the man that had stopped him.

Likely another person who wanted to catch up with him. James was a popular man in this town. He caught my eye and I gave him a reassuring smile. I enjoyed watching him interact with others, I enjoyed watching him at home.

"I am shocked that a lady like you is sitting here by yourself." I turned to see a man approach me, a smirk on his lips as he spoke.

"Only temporarily, just waiting for someone."

"Don't they know it's impolite to keep a beautiful lady waiting?"

"That's why he isn't keeping her waiting for long." James' voice appeared by my side, his hands wrapped protectively around my waist. There was no softness in his voice or gesture. He was making a claim. I was *his*.

He leant down and kissed me firmly. His slow, drugging kisses felt urgent as he moved his mouth with mine. Given that the man was still stood in front of us, it was incredibly obnoxious and I fucking loved it. His actions not only spoke to me, but to everyone else in the room. *Back off.*

"Nice to see you, Dexter," he said as he finally parted away from me. Dexter gave no response and walked to the other side of the bar.

"I never took you as a jealous man, Weatherston," I teased, placing my hand on his knee when he sat down.

"I wasn't one until I met you. Now, I can't stand the thought of anybody looking at you. It makes me want to gouge their eyes out."

Lucy

"James!" I couldn't hide the shock in my voice. "You can't say that."

"I'm only saying the truth. I saw the way Dexter was looking at you—he was one second away from that being the last thing he ever saw." I shook my head.

"You're trouble."

"And you love trouble," he said mockingly.

"I *really* love trouble." I felt a lurch of excitement when he looked at me. His eyes filled with desire as a smirk formed on his lips. Every time I looked at him, the pull was stronger and my feelings only grew deeper.

"I thought we were here to dance?"

"Don't pretend you want to dance; you just want an excuse to touch me."

"Guilty as charged." He laughed. "Although, I haven't heard you complaining about me touching you."

His eagerness to have his hands on me was a constant turn-on. He was going to have to wait a bit longer tonight. He had to earn it. Finishing my drink, I made my way to the dance floor. I didn't hold my hand out for him or give warning. I made my way solo to the floor and allowed the music to control my movements as my hands moved down my body.

James sat back in his chair, whiskey in hand.

His eyes watched me hungrily as he sipped his drink. It was like there was no one else in the room but the two of us. It was clear he was unable to keep still when he swigged the rest of his drink before heading over to me. His arms immediately found their way onto my body.

"Are you sure we can't go home yet?" he whispered in my ear in a way that made all the hairs on my neck stand up.

"Not yet," I teased. "You're going to dance with me first." He gave a mock salute before returning to his previous position.

We spent hours on that dance floor, we must have pretty much been the last people there. I didn't take much notice of anyone else. I was too busy enjoying every second in James' arms.

For a man who said he didn't have much time for dancing in his life, he was pretty good at it. He spun me around effortlessly, always matching my pace.

I could spend the rest of my life dancing with James Weatherston.

Thirty-Nine

James

So much had changed in the past few weeks I felt almost like a completely different person. In reality, this was the person I was supposed to be all along. I had spent years repressing who I was and living unhappily. I liked who I was now, I liked the person that Lucy had brought out of me.

I was quickly discovering that Lucy was not a morning person, especially after a night of drinking, dancing, and extra curriculars. I quietly untangled myself from her and headed to the kitchen. I was going to be on breakfast duty again and that was completely fine with me. I looked at the clock and saw it was after ten. As much as my body ached for more sleep, I needed to get back to the case. We had a good discussion and a list of suspects to work through. We were getting close, I could feel it. One of these leads would turn into something.

As I started brewing coffee, I heard the phone ringing, moving quickly to get it so it didn't wake Lucy in the other room. Very few people knew this number and I was happy when it was Daines on the other side.

"Hey, how is Lucy doing?" he asked immediately. It had only been just over a day since I'd seen him, but I was already missing talking to him.

Daines had always been the one constant in my life.

"She's okay, there's a lot of emotions brewing as you can imagine, but I'm doing my best to make her feel okay."

"You're a good man, James." I heard him take a deep breath. "Is she in ear-shot?" The question made me nervous.

"No, she's still sleeping, why?"

"I spoke to some of my friends who work at Kirkston City PD about her mother." I stayed quiet, desperate to hear what he found out. "Did Lucy mention anything about her mother being called to the station twice?"

"No. I know they went down to the station to make their statements together and that's when Lucy saw her father. She didn't go back there again afterwards. We went to the jail to see her dad the second time."

"Vera went back." The words swam round my brain. *Why did Vera go back? Why would they call her back in?* "She went back the next day, saw Anthony, and then changed her statement."

She saw Anthony.

Lucy had told me about how angry her mother had been that she saw her father. She made Lucy feel awful, but the next morning she went and saw him herself. Rage threatened to overwhelm me.

"Why did she change her statement? What was different?"

"They don't know exactly; apparently the original statement is gone. There is no record of the original anywhere when she and Lucy went together. Only the second one with the new

James

time stamp for the day after when she went again. My friend heard she gave the same statement, but changed her account on the timing of events that night."

"*Shit.* Thank you, Daines. Is Angie working tomorrow?" I needed to speak to Vera. I needed to know what happened. What was said between her and Anthony that made her change her statement?

"No, she doesn't work Tuesdays, why?"

"Do you think she would spend the day with Lucy for me? I want to go to talk to Vera in person if I can, but I don't want to leave Lucy alone with this guy still on the loose."

"Of course she would, it might be quite nice for the girls to spend the day together. I'll get her to call later."

"Thank you, I really appreciate your help with all this."

"Anytime, brother, you just call me." I thanked him and we ended the call. I knew Lucy had her aunt's number written down somewhere. It took me a second to locate it amongst all of our papers, but I raced back to the phone once I found it. The sound of a woman's voice answered the phone.

"Hey, can I speak to Vera Davis, please?" I tried to keep my voice soft, I didn't want them to think I was another reporter.

"Who is this?"

"James Weatherston, I'm the lawyer representing Anthony Davis." A deep sigh came from the other end of the phone.

"This is Vera, what can I do for you, James?" She didn't hang up on me, that was a good start.

"I have been reviewing lots of details about the case your daughter asked me to take on."

"I'm aware, of course. My daughter and I do speak, you know. She's told me that you were investigating things." *You've spoken to your daughter about twice,* I wanted to shout. *I know more about her feelings than you do.* I didn't say any of that, it wasn't good to reveal how close Lucy and I were.

"Of course." I tried to hide the sarcasm in my voice. "I have quite a few general questions that I need to ask you about Anthony. Just trying to work out the bigger picture here so I can see how this is all going to play out in trial."

"Well, you have about five minutes, so ask away."

"Actually, I was hoping we could meet. I understand you're staying out of town, so maybe we can meet halfway?"

"There is nothing you can ask me in person that you can't ask me on the phone," she said firmly.

"Arguably, I think these things are easier in person and five minutes is not enough time to establish the kind of man Anthony is."

"He's a fucking monster. Four minutes left, James." I was losing my grip on her.

"Vera, I need you to reconsider seeing me in person."

"Three minutes." Her voice was stern.

"I know you changed your statement." Suddenly she was silent.

"How do you know that…"

"I know a lot of things about you, Vera. Lots of things you wouldn't want anybody else to know." I was bluffing, but this was going to be the only way to grab her attention.

There was a pause on the other end of the line. "Tomorrow at noon," she finally said. I grinned as I wrote down the address of the diner she gave me. It was clear to me she was hiding a lot. I needed to see her in person to really get a good read on her.

"I'll see you tomorrow, Vera." She didn't respond as she hung up the phone. I only had to hope she actually showed.

Forty

Lucy

"Was that my mom on the phone?" I asked as I walked out into the kitchen. James looked a little startled at me appearing, like he had hoped I wouldn't overhear.

"Yeah, she's agreed to meet me tomorrow to talk things over."

"Where are we meeting her?" He looked at me shyly, bouncing between his feet.

"Actually, I am meeting her alone, Lucy." I couldn't help but feel sad as he spoke. A sense of rejection washed over me. "It's just that I think she will behave differently with you there."

He was right, of course, but part of me really wanted to see my mother. It had only been about a week, but it felt like ages since I had hugged her. Our relationship felt strained due to recent circumstances. Even though I knew she was hiding things, I still need my mom. I was desperate to feel some love from her.

"Daines said that Angie wanted to spend some time with you, so I thought you guys might be able to do something whilst I'm gone?"

"I don't need a babysitter, James." I rolled my eyes at him. I know he was worried about me, but I could be alone for five minutes. I wasn't a child.

"She's not babysitting you," he said with a laugh. "Daines and I just thought it would be nice for you two to spend some time together."

"Is that right?" I folded my arms across my chest.

"You are the two most important girls to us. Selfishly, we want you guys to have a friendship together."

"I know what you're doing, Weatherston."

"What's that?" he asked, raising an eyebrow teasingly.

"You're trying to sweet talk me into forgiving you for arranging it without asking me."

"Is it working?" he smirked.

"Luckily for you, yes." I leant up and gave him a kiss. "You can have my full forgiveness when I have a coffee in my hand." I had barely finished my sentence before he rushed to the kitchen, prompting me to laugh. As we sat down to have our coffees, I decided to quiz him more on the call.

"How did she sound?"

"I don't think she was particularly happy about receiving a call from your father's lawyer, but I think part of her was expecting it. She may have even thought it was weird that this was the first time I was reaching out."

"She probably assumed you had struggled to track her down," I countered. "Did she know about us?"

"No, I stuck to the same plan we had before. Act like the

Lucy

two of us hardly knew each other to make her see me as a complete third party." He looked at me before looking down at his hands. "She kind of made out like the two of you had spoken a lot and she knew everything about what I was doing."

"You're kidding?"

"Yeah, I guess she was playing on what you told her the other day, that you and I hardly communicated. She obviously assumed you hadn't told me to the two of you were hardly in contact." I fiddled nervously with the side of my cup as I thought about my mom. I wasn't at home anymore, so if she reached out after our call the other day, I wouldn't even know. Part of me knew she hadn't reached out; she wasn't exactly going to change her behaviour now.

"So, what's the plan?"

"I want to start it very similar to how you and I first spoke. Get her to tell me the history of her and your father. I imagine now we know about the affair, the things she will say will be different to how she might have spoken a few weeks ago before this all happened." I nodded. "Then we can go into more detail about her statement."

"About the timings?" James nodded.

"Daines called me this morning, your mother gave two statements." I looked at him confused, urging him to continue. "She made her first statement the day the two of you went together and then went the next day and changed it."

I couldn't believe what James was telling me.

My pride wanted to call him a liar, but I knew he wasn't. James would never lie to me. I saw my mother the next day, it was the day I went around, trying desperately to find a lawyer for Dad. She never mentioned the fact she went back to the station. I saw her that afternoon when she was packing to leave and she never said a word. Is that why she was in such a hurry to run away?

"Boss, there's more." James could clearly see my internal spiral as he looked nervous to speak. "She also saw your dad when she was there."

I put my hand over my mouth as I leant back in my chair, trying to take in what he had just told me. The *grief* that woman had given me over speaking to my father. She made me feel like a monster for even *considering* speaking to him. The number of tears I had shed because of how she made me feel and she went and saw him. James reached out his hand to me.

"I'm sorry, Lucy. I can't even begin to imagine how you feel."

"You're practically the only one in my life who doesn't owe me an apology, James." A sullen expression took over his face as he looked at me. "What did she change in her statement?"

"We don't know exactly; we're pretty certain it was her timing of events. The original statement is gone."

"Gone? You mean somebody got rid of it?"

"It seems to be that way, yes. There is no record of the statement she made when you came in together at all."

"Who would even get rid of it?" I remembered Detective Mason, the way he spoke to me when he interviewed me. I didn't know if he was also the one who spoke to my mom. We didn't talk about it afterwards. When I finished up with my dad, I sat in that waiting room for what felt like forever for my mother to come out. We were both so exhausted, we just wanted to go home and forget about the whole thing. I wished I had pressed her further now.

"That's what I am hoping to find out tomorrow. I have a lot of questions for your mother and she's going to give me

Lucy

answers," he said with a firmness in his voice.

"Well, then we better spend today preparing those questions." It was time to find out the truth.

Forty-One

James

Lucy and I spent the rest of the day going through files, pausing only for a dog walk and fresh air breather. I wanted to go into this conversation with Vera as prepared as possible. The lies ended here.

Angie had called in the evening to arrange a girls' day with Lucy. I was grateful for her and Daines, but I still felt conflicted about leaving Lucy. I was responsible for her safety and leaving her left me torn. I couldn't protect her if I wasn't right by her side. I knew that she would be safe, I'd called Daines whilst Lucy was in the shower last night to ask him to swing by and check on the girls during the day. It made it a little easier knowing he would be close by if anything went wrong.

The only thing pushing me to leave Lucy was wanting this all to come to a conclusion. Her mother was hiding something and I needed to prove it. Lucy was up unusually early this

James

morning when I rolled out of bed. I imagined the weight of today was heavy on her.

"Morning, beautiful," I said, coming up behind her in the kitchen. I wrapped my arms around her waist and kissed her cheek.

"How we feeling this morning?" she asked, clutching her hands around her coffee.

"Nervous," I admitted truthfully. I never felt the need to hide my feelings from her. "I just hope we get what we need to out of this conversation. I hope it'll help us figure out where to look next."

"If anyone can do it, it's you, James," she said softly.

* * *

A couple hours later, I was dressed and ready to head to meet Vera. I found myself hesitating by the door.

"I'll be fine, James. You don't need to worry about me," Lucy said, sensing my anxiety.

"You get in touch with Daines or head to the station if anything happens, okay?"

"Nothing is going to happen."

"Just promise me you'll be careful."

"I promise, now go because you're going to be late!" We embraced goodbye and I tried to settle my nerves.

"I love you, Lucy."

"Love you, too, good luck." It still felt surreal to hear Lucy tell me she loved me; I don't think there would ever come a time where it didn't make my heart flip.

I arrived at the diner ahead of Vera. Lucy had described her to me, so I knew who to look out for. A few moments later, as

I was starting to get worried that she wouldn't show, the door opened.

"James?" she asked as she walked over to me.

"That's me." I tried to give a reassuring smile; I didn't want her to find me threatening. Not yet, anyway. "You must be Vera. Was your drive okay?"

"I don't really want to bother with the small talk, if it's all the same to you." *Well, I guess that was how we're going to play this lunch.* We placed our order before getting down to talk.

"To start, I would like to talk about your relationship with Anthony. Can you describe your history for me?"

I listened as she took me on the journey of their relationship. As she spoke of how they met there was almost a hint of a smile on her lips. Clearly, even now, it was still a happy memory to her. Her expression slowly shifted to a frown as we progressed in time. His first affair was when she was pregnant with Lucy. Vera said she felt like she had no choice but to stay with him. He had many affairs over the years, so many that Vera didn't know all of them. She said he always promised he loved her *most* despite it. She knew she couldn't raise Lucy alone, so she stayed by his side.

"My mother always told me that's what I was supposed to do. Let him be free and play the dutiful wife, so I did." She sighed. "He was a good father and he kept a roof over our heads. I couldn't promise I'd have been able to do that without him."

"Did you still love him?"

"No," she said bluntly. "I stopped loving him when Lucy was about four. I would tell him I loved him, but I no longer meant it."

"Did you ever have an affair?"

"A few times," she said, nodding. "But I never would have if he hadn't first," she defended with a stern voice. She was desperate not to be portrayed as the villain.

"Do you think he killed Amber?"

"I know he did."

"You *know* he did? Did he confess to you when you saw him after his arrest?" Her face went white as a sheet. I guessed she thought she'd gotten away with her little visit.

"No, he never confessed, but I know my own heart, James. Do you trust your heart?"

"I do."

"So do I. And I know in my heart he killed that girl."

"What did you talk about when you saw him?"

"I wanted to say goodbye and good riddance," she said. The coolness in her tone put me on edge. "I wanted him to know I wouldn't miss him for a single minute. I hope he rots the rest of his life in that prison." *How did somebody so sweet come out of two people filled with so much anger and hate?*

"You changed your statement the day after you made the first one. Why did you do that?"

"I had forgotten some things that I thought were important to the case, some of my timings were off. I was under a lot of stress when we first heard about what he did and came to the station." Her hand twitched around her drink. She was nervous.

"You forgot or somebody asked you to change them?" Her eyes went wide as she looked at me.

"I don't know what you are accusing me of." Her voice raised slightly. I felt nearby tables turn to face us.

"It is not you I'm accusing—it's whoever asked you to change your statement. Did you know they destroyed your previous one? There's no record of it anywhere."

"They destroyed it? I guess that doesn't surprise me; my second statement looked a lot better for their case." She looked shocked; this part was true. Her guilt hearing that information was clear. "Nobody asked me to come back in; I did it of my own accord. They asked me a lot more questions and we edited the bits that I had gotten wrong."

"You said Anthony got home after midnight, is that true?"

"I don't know."

My mouth dropped. "You don't know?"

"I have no idea what time he got home. I never heard him come in that night. They needed me to say a time, so I said after midnight."

Anthony was adamant that he got home at ten-thirty. He was furious about the fact she had said midnight. It's because the whole time he was telling the truth.

"Why do you think they pushed you for a time?"

"Because they don't have a lot of evidence." I admired her honesty, I had been worried she would close off to me. "We all know he did it, but proving it was harder, so my statement would help send him down."

"Would you be willing to change your statement?"

"*Never.*" Harshness clouded her voice.

We talked a while longer as she explained more about herself and her childhood. I was surprised that she didn't once bring up Lucy. I would have thought a mother would be concerned about her child and her welfare in all of this. It struck me as odd that Lucy didn't even seem to cross her mind. Something still didn't feel right in all of this. I feel like both Vera and Anthony were giving me half the story.

"Thank you for taking the time to see me, Vera," I said as we

James

parted ways. "I will likely need to meet again after I have done some more digging. If you are right and Anthony is guilty, I'll drop the case." I didn't like the fakeness in my words, but I needed to keep Vera on side. If she knew what Lucy and I were up to, she would never agree to see me again. I still had to find the truth.

For now, I was going back to my car and back to Rosehaven. I couldn't wait to see Lucy again.

Forty-Two

Lucy

It didn't take me long to get over my initial worry about spending the day with Angie. She was one of the sweetest people I had ever met. She instantly made me feel welcome as we started to walk around the town. She listened so intently to everything I said and always had the right questions to ask. I know we had been half forced together by the two boys, but she never made me feel like a burden to her.

"I was thinking after we had a little shop around town, we could get our nails done?" she asked with a bright smile on her face.

"I don't think I've ever had my nails done before. My parents bought me some polish for my birthday a few years back, but I was never very good at it."

"Well, that is about to change," she said excitedly. "Maybe we can make it a bit of a thing, you and I having a girls' day and getting our nails done." There was something so genuine

Lucy

in the way she came across. This place felt more like home every day.

We walked into the first clothing store and began to look around. I had only packed a couple of days' worth of clothes and most of them were a random assortment I shoved in the bag in a rush. I wanted to find some more things to wear, maybe something to surprise James with. As we walked around, I couldn't help but notice somebody outside looking in. He had a hat and glasses on, so I couldn't see his eyes, but he seemed to be staring into the shop. Maybe I was overthinking it; there were men's clothes on display, too. It was perfectly reasonable for him to be looking in the window. Still, the paranoia ran through me.

"You okay?" Angie asked, coming up beside me.

"Yeah, just sometimes I feel like I'm being followed and I have to remind myself that nobody knows I'm here," I said lightly, trying to play off my fear.

"Do you want to go back? We can just spend the afternoon at the cabin if you'd rather."

"No! We have a whole day planned. I'm fine, I promise." I tried to get my head back into the day as I looked at a few more clothing options. When I looked up again, the man had walked slightly further down the street. He seemed to be looking in all of the stores, like he was looking for something specific, or maybe *someone*.

I looked out the window, trying to hide myself from view. It was his eyes I noticed as he took his sunglasses off. His dark, clouded eyes. The same eyes that had been knelt over me as hands clasped around my neck.

The man who tried to kill me was here. He'd found me.

The realisation made me fall to my knees with Angie rushing

Till Death Parts Us

to my side.

"Lucy, are you okay? What's going on?" Initially, I was in too much shock to speak as the store assistant rushed over, too.

"It's him, Angie, he's here." Her eyes widened, immediately knowing what I was talking about.

"Come on, the station is down the road. We need to find Daines." She helped me to my feet and looked at the door, watching as he walked into a nearby store. "Come on, now." She grabbed my head and hurried me out the door. I was glad I had her by my side, but I suddenly longed for James.

"Hey, baby," Daines said to Angie as we were brought into the office where he was. His expression immediately dropped when he saw the state I was in. "What happened?" I found myself unable to speak again as Angie directed me towards a chair.

"The man who attacked Lucy, he's here." Angie spoke where I wasn't able to.

"Where?" Daines sounded panicked.

"He was on the high street just now."

"I need you to tell me what he looked like." The calmer Daines who was here before was long gone and he seemed ready to jump to action.

"What are you going to do?" I asked, finally finding my voice.

"I just want to find out what he is up to and who he is." We had no proof of what he did to me, so it wasn't like Daines could arrest him. Angie began describing the man in detail, including his outfit.

"Both of you need to stay right here until I get back, don't you dare move." I had no interest in moving; this police station was going to be the safest place for me until James was here. *God, I wished James was here.*

Daines was probably only gone ten minutes, but it felt like hours. Angie sat next to me and held my hand. Multiple people offered us drinks, but I couldn't bear to do anything other than sit. A wave of anxiety hit me when Daines came back through the door.

"What happened?" Angie asked.

"Nothing, I just talked to him." He sat down opposite me.

"About me?" He shook his head.

"No, I just made polite conversation—asking him what he was up to today, that sort of thing." He took a deep breath. "His name is Carter; said he was in town visiting family. He's the kind of guy I would have called nice had I not known about what he did," Daines said, as if he was almost ashamed of himself. "I got his licence plate as he drove away, too."

"What do we do now?" Angie asked.

"I have an hour left on my shift, I'm going to run the plate and try to find out as much information about him as possible. You ladies are going to stay here until my shift is finished and then we are going to go back to the cabin together and wait for James."

"What are we going to do when we find out who he is?" Angie followed up.

"I'll have to wait for James, he'll know what to do." I couldn't help but agree with Daines.

James would know how to handle this.

Forty-Three

James

As I walked back into the cabin, I was immediately greeted with Lucy running over to me. At first, I was overjoyed until I saw the look on her face. As I scanned the room, I noticed Daines and Angie sitting with similar looks on their faces.

"What happened?" I asked, swallowing the lump in my throat.

"He's here," Lucy said as she stepped away from me.

"Who?" My mind went through a few different options as I waited for her response.

"The guy who attacked me." I felt my knees weaken at her words. "Angie and I were in town just shopping around and we saw him."

"What happened? Did he hurt you?" I felt my voice begin to raise. "Where is he now?" My eyes shot to Daines, hoping his presence meant he did something about this.

James

"He didn't touch me; he didn't know we were there," Lucy reassured.

"But he was looking for you," Angie interjected.

"We don't know that for certain. He told Daines he was in town visiting family, it could be coincidence," Lucy countered.

"Of course, he told me that. I'm a police officer in uniform—he's not exactly going to tell me he's in town hunting women." Daines' tone was harsh and I gave him a warning glance. He was my friend, but he didn't get to speak to her like that.

"You spoke to him?" My question was aimed at Daines as I held onto Lucy protectively.

"Briefly. Found out his name was Carter and got his licence plate. I ran them through the system when I got back. His name is Carter Jones." He paused. "…He's Amber's father, he has previous record for violence, so I'm not surprised he was seeking revenge. He's a rough guy."

A stab of guilt hit my chest, I had left Lucy and this is what happened. I was grateful he didn't touch her, but I never should have left her alone. Not whilst he was still out there walking about. I knew he was grieving his daughter, but that didn't make it okay for him to hurt the woman I loved. Nothing would ever make it okay. He needed to be punished.

"Did he say how long he was staying in town for?" Daines shook his head.

"Why? What are you going to do?" Lucy asked.

"I don't know." That was the truth, I had so much information going through my brain right now I needed time to process. I was hoping to come home and start thinking about all the information Vera had given me, but that needed to be put aside for tonight. Lucy was in danger and that was my top priority. "But I will be doing something, I just need time to think, that's all."

"We don't have any proof, James; we don't even have proof he is in town after me." I knew that, but I wasn't going to let a little thing like lack of proof stop me. This was Lucy's safety we were talking about. I was suddenly angry at myself that I didn't make her go to the police when it first happened. It never should have gotten this far.

"Lucy, I know you know it isn't a coincidence he is in town." My gaze was hard as I looked at her. Her eyes softened and I knew deep down she agreed. Maybe she was just too scared to admit it out loud. I guess if I was in danger, I may be scared to admit it, too. "He isn't going to come anywhere near you. I promised you I'd keep you safe and I meant it. I need you to promise me you won't go anywhere without either Daines and I." I eyed Daines briefly and he nodded. I didn't need to ask his permission to take care of her.

"I promise. I think I want to just stay here for a bit. This cabin kind of feels like the safest place to be." I nodded.

"We should probably get going, unless you need me?" Daines interjected.

"Let me walk you both out. Why don't you go relax, boss, and I'll make you some dinner." Lucy thanked them both and cuddled up on the sofa with Cato as I walked Angie and Daines outside.

"I'll meet you in the car, sweetheart," Daines said to Angie. I waved her goodbye as she walked towards the car. "So, what's the plan then, Weatherston?"

"What do you mean?" I questioned, even though I knew exactly what he meant.

"What are we going to do about Carter? I know the wheels are turning in that head of yours. He's not going to stop until he gets her." I swallowed hard. I knew that and it was the only thought that had run through my brain since I walked through the door.

"I have a plan," I said, purposely keeping my response short.

"Care to share?"

"You're an officer of the law," I said, half teasing. "I don't want to involve you in something that could jeopardise your career." I had come to terms with the fact my career was essentially over before it had even begun. I wasn't going to take Daines' away from him, too.

"James, I want you to involve me. I would do anything for you and I am not going to let this man walk around town. I have a duty to protect the people here and Lucy. Whatever your plan is, I'm in."

"Are you a hundred percent sure? If we got caught…" I trailed off.

"I am all in, James."

"Can you meet me later?" His eyes wandered to Angie in his car and then back to me.

"Yeah, when Angie is asleep, I'll come back."

"You remember that spot we always used to hang out at?" He nodded. "Meet me there, keep your lights off when you get close." Wandering back in, I passed Lucy, giving her a kiss on the forehead before heading to the kitchen to make her something to eat. My only goal for tonight was to make Lucy feel as safe and secure as possible. I wanted her to go to bed in my arms forgetting about everything that was going on. Then, when she was asleep, Carter Jones would pay for what he did to her.

Forty-Four

Lucy

James more or less refused to leave my side for a moment the rest of the evening. He was on high alert, I could tell. He waited in the bedroom when I was having a shower. It made me feel safe that he was watching over me, but that man was still in the back of my mind. *Carter Jones.* I tried to convince myself he wasn't here for me, but James was right. There was no coincidence in his appearance here. I just had to hope he didn't know about the cabin or about James' link to me. As I fell asleep, James cuddled me close, whispering sweet words in my ear. It was my new favourite way to fall asleep.

Unfortunately, it did nothing to stop the nightmares and a few hours later, I was awake again. Although this time, James wasn't there to comfort me. He wasn't in the room at all. As I sat up, I noticed Cato was still in the room, but no James. Looking towards the bathroom, I couldn't see a light on there,

Lucy

either.

"James?" I called out, but no response came back.

As I got myself up and started heading towards the bedroom door, I heard the front door close. I backed away to the bed, scared that someone had just entered the house. The bedroom door opened and James walked through. An immediate sigh of relief left me.

"Oh my God, you scared me."

"Sorry, Lucy." He was taking his jacket off as he walked through the door.

"Where were you?" I questioned. He was clearly dressed for outside and not in the clothes he had gone to bed in.

"I couldn't sleep, just had so much on my mind so I went for a walk around the lake. I didn't want to wake you up. I didn't mean to scare you."

"I know you didn't. Are you okay?" I asked, sitting on the edge of the bed as I turned the lamp on. He came and sat next to me.

"Yeah, just feel like I have too much to think about, that's all. I needed some fresh air after today."

"Oh, the meeting with my mother." With everything that happened yesterday, I had almost forgotten why James wasn't with me in the first place. "How did that go?"

"Lucy, it's late. Are you sure you don't want to wait till morning to talk about it?"

"I doubt I'll be able to go back to sleep for a while. Can we talk about it now?" If he had just gone for a walk, I doubted he was in the mood to go straight to sleep. This was one of those conversations I wanted over with. Now it was on my mind, it wasn't going anywhere.

"She was surprisingly forward with me about everything."

Till Death Parts Us

He shifted himself so he was leaning on the headboard. "It took a little pushing, but she spoke about going to visit your dad. She said she did it to say goodbye, to tell him that he got what he deserved, basically."

Those words were hard to hear, but I was glad I could trust James to be honest with me. I felt like I had heard so many negative things recently that these were starting to bounce off me now. I didn't have any more energy to give to my emotions.

"What about the fact she changed her statement?"

"She said that she had missed some things and went back in to change them. She admitted she lied about the time your father got in." His eyes looked tired as he pressed on. "She didn't actually know what time he got in."

"She didn't know what time Dad got home? He could have been home by ten-thirty like he said? James, that's fantastic! We just need to get her to retract that from her statement."

"She said she would never change her statement." My heart dropped. I forgot how stubborn my mother was. Of course it wasn't going to be that easy.

"What do we do now?"

"I'm not sure. I need some time to think things over tomorrow. I doubt it will be the last conversation your mother and I have." He wiped his eyes with his hands. "Let's go to bed, Lucy, at least try to sleep."

"Okay." I nodded as I shuffled myself over back to my side of the bed. "James?" He looked at me as he laid down. "Do you mind if we go back to my house tomorrow? I had intended to get some more clothes in town with Angie today, but with everything going on I think I'd just rather go home and pack some more things."

"Of course, sweetheart, we'll head over in the morning." He

Lucy

kissed my head before turning the lamp off.

***

I felt nervous as James' car approached my old house. I didn't feel like calling it a home anymore. The cabin felt more like my home than this place did. I hadn't really even thought of my house since we left that night, how scared I was cowering behind the door waiting for James to arrive. My intention was to pack things as quickly as I could and get out of there.

"Do you want me to go and pack some stuff for you?" James offered, sensing my nerves.

"No, thank you, I can do it." My eyes scanned my surroundings and there wasn't a reporter in sight. They had obviously realised both my mother and I had moved out for the time being. Their story had gone elsewhere.

I unlocked the front door and was immediately hit with memories as I opened it. Memories of the fear I felt coming back from that walk where Carter had attacked me.

As I walked through, I saw the pictures on the wall. I remembered looking at them when the police officer was here and being suddenly aware how fake the smiles from my parents were. The more I found out about their marriage, the faker these smiles appeared. They had been putting on an act since the moment I was born.

"Do you mind if I nose around whilst you pack?" James asked. I don't know what he had hoped to find. Whilst the officer had been talking to my mother and I initially, another couple officers had searched my parents' bedroom. Other than the sleeping pills, they found nothing of value. If my parents had things to hide, they were hidden well.

"Of course." I left him to snoop as I headed to my bedroom to pack up as much as I could. I didn't want to return here in a rush.

Forty-Five

James

My plan for Carter Jones was fully in action and there was no going back now. My only regret was not telling Lucy the truth about what I was doing out of bed. I knew she would find out eventually, but for now, I wanted to keep it close to my chest. I felt lighter the next day knowing what was in hand. He wouldn't be a problem anymore and Lucy could go to sleep easier soon enough.

I immediately found my way into her parents' bedroom and started looking around. Vera had taken a lot of stuff with her, so it was mostly just Anthony's stuff left behind. It made me feel like Vera didn't plan on coming back anytime soon. I wonder if her thought process was to leave until after the trial. If she knew she was lying about her statement, she wouldn't want to take the stand. She gave the information up so easily, I was sure I would have gotten it out of her at the trial. I imagine she knew that, too, and wanted to keep away. As Anthony's wife, legally, she didn't have to testify. Did she plan on using that to her advantage?

What was her plan if Anthony went to prison? If it were me, I'd never want to live in these walls again if my husband went down for murder. The memories leaked out of the walls here; there seemed to be an obsession in this family with photos. Every single room you walked through there were multiple photos of the family. Don't get me wrong, my parents had a lot of photos, too, but this was taking it to the next level. It was almost like they had something to prove.

I guess they did in the end. Vera had lived her entire life with Lucy having to fake everything. I am not surprised knowing what I do now that Lucy was an only child. Vera probably felt bad enough bringing one child into an unhappy marriage. These photos were clearly a coping mechanism for Vera, that is why they were so over the top. There was no real happiness in this family, so she had to make believe.

She wanted anybody who walked into this house to think that this family was a completely normal family. She had been desperate to stop the cracks from showing. It was sad, when you really thought about it; the effort Vera went to pretend everything was okay. It must have worked well, as Lucy seemed none the wiser to her parents' plight. Truthfully, I don't know how they managed to keep the facade up all of these years. It was impressive, to say the least.

It still didn't excuse her lying in her statement. Just because he had affairs, didn't mean he deserved to spend the rest of his life in prison. I know she claimed she did it because she believed he was guilty. When I looked at her, none of her words seemed to ring true completely. There were still pieces missing from this puzzle .

James

After a while, I gave up looking through the bedroom as there was nothing here to see. Next, I headed to Anthony's office. It struck me as a little odd that he even had an office. Neither of the jobs he was working at the time of his arrest required any kind of home office. Maybe because they never had any more children, it was just a spare room that needed filling. There was a phone connected in this room—maybe this is where he would come to talk to the women he was having an affair with privately.

I went through all of the drawers, hoping to come across something good, but there was nothing. There were plenty of bills and financial papers that showed their financial issues, but I already knew this. Lucy had been open about the family money struggles. It was lucky she had gotten a scholarship or she would never have been able to go to even the local college.

Just as I was about to give up and go and find Lucy, a floor board squeaked oddly beneath my feet. I walked around again to test the others around it. This was an old house, after all. The squeak came again and I bent down to investigate it further. I realised it was loose and started to tug it. It was a little stiff, but it came up a lot easier than it should have.

My eyes widened with what I was met with underneath. *Jackpot.* I gathered everything up, placing it carefully in my bag. I think Vera and I needed to have another conversation. I no longer had time for games.

Forty-Six

Lucy

After leaving my house, James told me he wanted to meet my mother again the next day and asked me how I felt being with Daines for the day. I found it sweet that he would ask me before making the decision. I could tell he was anxious to keep working on the case, but he put my feelings before his own. He always had my safety at the forefront.

I didn't know what else he had to ask my mother, but I agreed to spend the day with Daines nonetheless. As long as I wasn't on my own, I was happy. He called my mother in the afternoon and they agreed to meet at the same place. He told me he wanted to ask her questions about the trial itself that he had been regretting not asking her before.

When I asked him if he thought my father's case was going to trial, he pulled a strange expression. I wasn't sure exactly how to read him, but he just said *hopefully not*.

Lucy

Daines was working the next day, so they agreed I would stay at the police station until James returned. It wasn't ideal, but I had picked up some books to read at my house so I had plenty to keep me entertained.

James waved over to Daines and Angie as we walked in, but Daines' expression was panicked.

"I thought you were coming at ten?" His eyes were wide as he looked at James.

"We were ready early, so I figured we'd come down," James replied as a frustrated look crossed Daines' face. Before he could explain himself, there was a commotion at the front. I watched as Carter Jones was dragged in by three police officers, his hands bound with cuffs. Confusion hit me and I looked at James. He didn't seem surprised at all. In fact, he almost seemed happy.

"I didn't do anything!" Carter yelled as they dragged him through the station. He was clearly trying to thrash about, but the officers kept their grip tight on him. As they pulled him past me, our eyes met and his widened. He knew exactly who I was and as fear overcame me, he knew that I knew who he was, too. Those dark eyes focused on me and I felt like I was back in that park. James moved closer, wrapping an arm around me. Carter didn't shout again, but his eyes stayed on me, hatred consuming them. He didn't take them off me until he no longer had a choice. My entire body ran cold.

"What is he in for?" I asked Daines, his shiftiness when we first walked in still had my attention. It was almost like he knew Carter was going to come through that door.

"He was found with drugs in his car, it seems he must have been some kind of dealer." Daines spoke as if he was unsure in what he was saying. His eyes kept darting to James.

"Did he have a previous record for drugs? I know you said he was violent, but I don't remember drugs."

"No, I guess it was a new thing for him," Daines said with a shrug. I wasn't convinced; there was a knowing look shared between the two men that made me uneasy.

"You set him up." The words were out of my mouth before I could stop them. James looked at me and his eyes told me everything.

"He deserves everything he is getting, Lucy. He is not a nice man, he tried to kill you." James was trying to excuse himself, but it didn't make me any less angry.

"What did you do?"

"We planted the drugs." I saw Angie shoot Daines a look out of the corner of my eyes. She wasn't aware of their plan, either. "We knew we would never get him for what he did to you, but I couldn't let him walk around any longer."

"The night you first saw him, we put them in his car and waited a couple of days before calling an anonymous tip in. A couple other officers pulled him over today."

"What if they found out it was the two of you?" Angie asked in a hushed tone, joining my interrogation.

"They won't, we were careful." It made sense now—James' early morning walk. He wasn't clearing his head, he was setting up Carter.

"His daughter was just murdered, don't you think he has been through enough?" I asked, directing my attention towards James.

"No," James said, no hesitation in his voice. "If I am honest, I don't think the few years he will get for this is enough. I meant what I said, Lucy. There isn't *anything* I wouldn't do for you."

Forty-Seven

James

My whole body relaxed at the sight of Carter Jones being dragged through in cuffs. I had nervously waited for this since the other night.

My original plan was to beat the shit of him, but Daines talked me down. Plan B was to get him arrested with something that would mean he would go to prison for a couple of years. A couple of years wasn't enough, but it was something. I needed to see him suffer for what he did to Lucy. He nearly took the most important thing in my life away from me. I wasn't going to give him the opportunity to do it again.

I only had to hope that in a couple of years this whole ordeal with Amber Jones would be over and he wouldn't come for Lucy ever again. If he did, then there was nothing Daines could say that would stop me going back to plan A. There wasn't anything I wouldn't do for Lucy.

I had never intended to hide it from her for long, just long enough that it was too late for her to stop me. Lucy was a good person. Even though he made her suffer, she would let it go. Even though she now spent her nights scared, she would still let it go.

I would never be able to let it go.

It took her mere seconds to uncover what we had done; she was incredibly intuitive. I just hoped she loved me enough to forgive me, to realise I did this for her, not because I'm some monster. Going around getting people arrested wasn't exactly my forte.

"James, there is still time to take it back." Lucy looked at me in a way that broke my heart. I didn't want her to be angry with me.

"I won't take it back, Lucy."

Tears brimmed her eyes, making me feel even more guilty. She then looked at Daines.

"It had to be done, Lucy-Lou." Daines never once hesitated in helping me. I figured when we came up with the plan he would want to walk away, but he was determined. I don't know what I did to deserve a friend like him. She went quiet and looked resigned, her eyes looking at the new empty space where Carter had been dragged through.

I could tell her thoughts were conflicted.

"Sometimes, justice isn't black and white, Lucy. I had to operate on a grey area on this one. We would never have been able to prove he hurt you and there was no way in hell I was going to let him hurt you again."

"James is right," Angie interjected. "I don't agree with what you two did, but I get it." Her eyes darted between Daines and I. Daines looked at the floor, avoiding her gaze. I just hoped this didn't cause repercussions for them. "Do you think it was a coincidence he was here in town, Lucy? He was hunting you; he was going to kill you. We all just saw the way he looked at you. He wasn't going to stop until you were dead." Her last word clung to the air like a putrid smell.

She sighed; I could tell she knew that was true.

"I just don't remember Mystery Incorporated framing people for crimes they didn't commit." A collective laugh came from all of us which felt unnatural for the moment.

"Maybe I need to resign my title of Fred, then," Daines said with a shrug.

"I don't think I'm deserving of it anymore." I raised my hands in jest. I turned my full attention to Lucy. "I'm not sorry for what I did, but I am sorry for not including you in the decision."

"It's going to take me some time to process this." I nodded. "I guess I don't need to be here anymore since he's locked up. I think I'm going to go back to the cabin and get some fresh air."

"I'll drive you back."

"No, you need to get on to see my mother. I think the time apart wouldn't hurt." My heart felt crushed at her words.

"I'll take you," Angie said, moving towards Lucy. The two said goodbye to Daines and started walking away.

"I love you, Lucy." I couldn't let her go without her hearing these words. She turned back to face me.

"I love you, too." Her voice was weak, but she still loved me.

"You can yell at me, be angry with me, you can hit me all you want if you need to, but please don't stop loving me."

"I don't think I could ever stop loving you, James." With those words, the two were gone.

"Everything will be okay," Daines said, gripping my shoulder.

"Will it?" My nerves were shot.

"They'll be angry at us for a while, but they will come round eventually. We did what we had to do and the world is safer with that man off the street. Even before he attacked Lucy, he wasn't exactly a good man. We did the right thing."

I wished Daines' words reassured me, but in this moment, all I could do was worry that I was going to lose Lucy. I couldn't bear the thought of losing her. Alongside keeping the Carter secret, I had one more secret. I only hoped this one didn't blow up in my face and that I would lose her forever.

"You need to go, James." Daines broke me from my thoughts. "I reckon solving this case and freeing her father from prison will go a long way in her forgiving you."

He was right, I had work to do.

Forty-Eight

Lucy

I felt a little bad for Angie having to sit in a car with me in my current state. My brain was overwhelmed with emotions and I could barely hold a conversation. When I shut down her attempts to talk about the situation, she then tried to make polite conversation. Even then I struggled to entertain it. When I was calm, I would apologise to her for my harshness.

"Do you want me to come in with you?"

"No, thank you." I gave her a weak smile. "I just want to process all this on my own for a bit." She nodded, but she looked unsure. She reached into her driver's side and started writing on a piece of paper.

"Here is my number. If you change your mind, I'll just be at home all day. Even if you want me to just come sit in silence with you, that is totally fine." I took it off her graciously and said goodbye.

Briefly, I thought about how good she and Daines were together. They were two of the most selfless people I knew. They always seemed to be willing to do things for other people all the time without a fuss. They were perfect for each other, I just hoped they made it out of this situation unscathed. Daines had hid this from her, as well.

I was greeted by an excited Cato as I made it through the door. Now that the town was safe, I thought it a good time to walk and feel my emotions. It was colder by the water today, so I grabbed one of James' jackets off the side. The smell of him was encompassed in it and I immediately felt comfortable. It was incredible how even the smell of someone you loved made you feel safe.

I knew in my heart I would forgive James, we would make it out of this. He was trying to protect me, I knew that. I saw Carter Jones' crime sheet when Daines first found it. He was a violent and horrid man. I wouldn't have put it past him to be the kind of father who beat Amber when she was younger. His whole presence made me shudder.

My thoughts fell to Amber. She was a lot younger than my father, so it begged the question what did she see in him? Having seen the kind of man her father was, I imagined there was not much love as a child. Maybe she was trying to replace some fatherly love she never got to have with my Dad. It was twisted when you thought about it.

What did my father see in her? He claims he loved her. James admitted to me that my mother said my dad's affairs started very early on. It begs the question, did my father ever love my mother? Did he have all of those affairs because he was desperate to be loved?

As people, I feel we are always searching for love wherever

we can get it, even if it is a small dose. We thrive off of it. I know that even despite the heartbreak of my situation, James' love has pulled me through all of it. Without his love, I am not sure I would have survived this situation. I would have just become a shell of myself.

I hoped I never knew a world without James' love again.

The thoughts of my father made me feel guilty. I hadn't made any attempt to call or see him since the last time. I had been so wrapped up in what I was trying to do, I forgot who I was doing it all for.

When I returned to the cabin, I put a call into the prison. I had no idea what I was supposed to do. The lady who answered took the number and said phone time was in an hour, so she would get my father to call.

The next hour was excruciatingly slow whilst I waited. It would still be a while till James was home and I had to figure out what I was going to say to my father. I jumped when the phone finally rang.

"Lucy?" It felt strangely nice to hear my father's voice again.

"Dad, how are you doing?" I could feel his hesitation before responding through the phone.

"I'm okay, sweetheart. How are you doing?" This phone call felt like a stark contrast with my mother; I didn't have to ask him to check on me.

"I'm good." I didn't know if that was the truth or not. It was probably a lie. "Been helping that lawyer, James, a lot on the case." I had no reason to hide my relationship with James from my father, but it just happened naturally. I would tell him after we proved his innocence.

"How is that all going?"

"Better than I thought," I answered honestly. "We aren't

there yet, but I feel like we have some good leads to follow. I'm doing everything I can, Dad, I promise."

"I knew you would." There was a hint of a smile in his voice. "You are the best daughter I could have asked for."

"I'm your only daughter." I laughed.

Our conversation continued until he was told he had to get off the phone. We spoke about what it was like in prison. I didn't bother to tell him about Carter. I didn't need him to know what happened to me. I did, however, talk to him about my mother. He was angry that she had left town without me, calling her names I had never heard him say before. It was funny how obvious the strain in their marriage was now, I don't know how I never saw it before.

We ended the conversation with a promise to talk again. I told him I was staying with a friend, so he should use this number instead. He seemed to buy it quite easily.

Now all I had to do was sit and wait for James. I could only hope he brought with him a breakthrough.

Forty-Nine

James

I just figured out who killed Amber Jones and it is going to tear the person I love's life apart.

Fifty

Lucy

I heard the soft closing of the front door and immediately made my way to the living room. My heart dropped at the sight of him. His eyes were red like he had been crying on the drive home. He offered me a weak smile as he caught sight of me.

"Evening, boss." His voice was shaky as he walked over to the table, putting his stuff down.

"James?" I approached him slowly; tears brimmed his eyes again as I got close to him. I hadn't seen him like this before, he was usually the one having to comfort me. I pulled him into a hug and he let out a quiet sob as he put his hand on the back of my head.

"I'm so sorry, Lucy." *Was he just upset about earlier?*

"James, I forgive you for Carter. I know you were only doing what you thought was best for me." He lifted his head up and shook it.

Lucy

"That's not what I'm sorry for." I felt my breathing get faster with anticipation.

"What's happened, James?"

"I need you to sit down, Lucy."

"James, you're scaring me." He didn't respond, only gesturing for me to sit down. Once I did, he sat across from me, pulling a tape recorder out of his bag.

"I need you to know that whatever you want to do after hearing this, I am okay with. I will deal with the consequences." His hand hovered shakily over the play button before he pushed it down.

* * *

Audio Recording between Vera Davis and James Weatherston

James: What can you tell me about all these photos of women I found in your husband's office?

Vera: I have never seen these before.

James: I don't have the patience to play games, Vera. You see, when I found them, they looked like they'd been tossed in anger under the floorboards. Next to them was this box, which I assume is where they were kept neatly before. Did it make you angry when you found these photos?

Vera: Are you deaf? I have never seen those before.

James: These are pictures of women he has had an affair with, I'm assuming? I imagine he took all of these. I don't think he would have tossed all these lovely photos angrily. These seem to go back years. Does it make you angry that he kept these like trophies?

Vera: What if Lucy had found them? How was I supposed to explain all of this to her? I can't believe he was stupid enough to keep these photos in the house.

James: So, you admit to knowing about these photos?

Vera: Yes, I knew about the photos.

James: How do these make you feel?

Vera: Angry, of course. Anyone in their right mind would be angry about this.

James: Angry enough to want revenge?

Vera: I don't know what you are suggesting, but I do not have to sit here and listen to this.

James: Please sit down. I'm just asking a question; did you feel vengeful towards your husband?

Vera: Sometimes.

James: Vera, how did Amber Jones die?

Vera: My husband strangled her to death.

James: No, he didn't. I'll ask you again. How did Amber Jones die?

Vera: I had nothing to do with it.

James: It was actually something Lucy said to me that made me realise it wasn't Anthony. She told me she thought it was strange that her father would use sleeping pills to help himself overpower Amber. As you know, your husband is a large man, why would he need them? He could easily have overpowered Amber.

James: That's when I thought, maybe it wasn't a man at all. Maybe it was a woman who killed Amber. We talked a lot of jealousy killing and I thought to myself, who is going to be the most jealous about the fact Amber and Anthony were in love? I settled on you.

Vera: He didn't love her, that man wasn't capable of loving anyone.

Lucy

James: He told me himself that he loved her, he was planning on starting a new life with her. Did you know that?

Vera: Bullshit!

James: Did you kill Amber Jones?

James: Vera, it's time for the truth. Did you kill her?

Vera: Yes…I didn't have a choice.

James: You killed her so your husband couldn't have her? Is that it?

Vera: No, I killed her so he could rot in prison for the rest of his life. That is what he deserves.

James: Did Amber deserve to die?

Vera: It was for the greater good, one life to help many others.

James: I think it would be a good idea to go down to the station, don't you? Anthony doesn't deserve to be locked up for something he didn't do.

Vera: Why would I do that? There is no proof that I did this, my statement will help put Anthony away for life. Nobody will ever be able to find any evidence I did this, I was careful.

James: I guess you're right, no one will ever have proof you killed Amber.

END OF RECORDING

***

My head felt light as the recording ended. I felt like I might pass out. *My mother was a killer.* I didn't know how to process this, but I heard her say it herself. She admitted to it.

"She didn't know she was being recorded?" James shook his head. "How did you know it was her?"

"It was a hunch. When I went to see your father, he was angry that she had said he wasn't home till late. He started saying something then stopped. It occurred to me he was going to say that your mother wasn't even there when he got home."

"Because she was at Amber's house." It had almost seemed like a joke when we wrote my mother on the suspect list. There was nothing funny about it now. "What do we do?"

"What do you want to do?" I was so shaken by the events I couldn't even cry. The past few days had seemingly used all of my tears. "It's down to you what we do with this information, Lucy."

"I don't know what to do." I didn't want to have to make this decision.

"You don't have to decide till tomorrow, you can sleep on it first. We either hand this tape in, or we destroy it and leave your father exactly where he is." He took a breath. "Either way, I'll be right behind you, Lucy. I'll support you no matter what."

The weight on my shoulders was heavy as I sat down trying to process this information. I knew there was no way I would be getting any sleep tonight.

I had two choices. Give that tape to the police which would prove my father's innocence and send my mother to jail instead. Alternatively, we destroyed the tape and allowed my mother's plan to play out and my father spends the rest of his life in prison for something he didn't do. He had spent their whole marriage having affairs, but did that justify Amber dying and him being in prison? It just didn't make sense why she would do something so drastic to get revenge?

The next morning, I was still wide awake as James sat up

Lucy

next to me.

"I want to give the tape to the police," I said before he spoke.

"Are you sure?" I nodded.

I hoped I was making the right decision here.

Fifty-One

James

Whilst I had hoped Lucy would give the tape into the police, I was also just as willing to destroy it if she asked. The whole drive home from my talk with Vera I cried. Not because I felt any sympathy for her or Anthony, but because of Lucy. I cried because I knew this was going to tear her apart. Where I always wanted to be the person bringing her comfort, in this case, I was bringing her pain. I hated the fact the tears on Lucy's face were caused by something I was bringing her.

I didn't tell her why I was meeting her mother truthfully, because I wasn't sure I was right. It was a hunch more than anything else. I didn't want to upset Lucy unnecessarily by accusing her mother of being a killer without my facts being straight.

Unfortunately, my hunch was correct and now we were taking the drive out to Kirkston PD. I had called ahead to the

James

police station to let them know what I found. We would go there and show them the tape. There was no doubt in my mind they would go to arrest her straight away. This was a big case and they wouldn't want to be seen faltering on it. We would wait in the station for her mother to be brought in. I imagine the officers will have a lot of questions for us, too.

I didn't bother asking Lucy if she was okay, I knew she wasn't. I allowed her to lead the conversation as we drove and she chose to steer away from her family. Instead, she talked about the future, *our future.* It felt slightly odd to be discussing it now but I was desperate to provide her with some comfort.

"I know we can't stay in that cabin forever, but do you think we could find somewhere to live in Rosehaven?"

"Of course." I wasn't saying that to appease her, I had been thinking about it ever since we came here. How much I missed being home. I had never felt that feeling of home in Kirkston City, I'd missed it. I wanted to make a home with Lucy, too. I wanted both of us to get a fresh start after all of this was over. I could commute for work in the city if I needed to.

As we arrived at the station, we were greeted by Detective Mason.

I did not allow him to take Lucy from my side as we were led into a room. They listened to the tapes and immediately put a warrant out for Vera's arrest. I knew it would be a few hours till she was transferred over from here since she was out of town. We decided to go to visit Anthony at the prison whilst we waited and we'd come back to the station after. He would not be released until she was charged, but he could at least hear the good news.

"Lou!" he said as he was brought into the room. "One of the guards just told me they would be releasing me soon."

Till Death Parts Us

Excitement filled his eyes. I guess the good news got here faster than we could. The guard didn't stop him as he hugged Lucy. This was the first time I had seen Lucy cry since she listened to the tape yesterday. She hugged her father tightly as she allowed the sobs to come out. He started to break down, too, and I felt a little bit like I shouldn't be here for this.

As he pulled away, he made his way over to me, pulling me into a hug, too. It was unexpected and I didn't know what to do with myself at first. He wouldn't be hugging me like that if he knew the stuff I was doing with his daughter whilst he was in prison.

I guess the emotion of the moment had gotten to him. I couldn't even begin to imagine how it felt to be in prison for something you didn't do. To live in fear every day you would be here for the rest of your life when you did nothing wrong.

"Do you know when I'm getting out?" He looked at me expectantly.

"When Vera has been charged. She's about five hours out of town, but I imagine she's on her way to Kirkston now. As soon as she's in custody and charged with Amber's murder, they will release you. You'll need to stay in town for a while." I looked over at Lucy. "Unfortunately, this is far from over."

Anthony may be free, but we now had Vera's case to go. Vera being guilty meant the whole family would still have to go through the ordeal of a trial. The media would be all over this the second the story broke. It would probably be bigger than the Murray case. It had been a few days since I had thought about that case. The trial would have begun by now and I wasn't in that courtroom I worked so hard to sit in with. I should feel sad, but I'm almost relieved. I think I need to take a break after this one. Lucy was going to need my support

James

during this trial and I wanted to give her as much of my time as I could.

"I can't wait to be out of here," he said, rubbing his hands over his face. "I want to testify against Vera." The words shocked me initially, but I guess it made sense.

"I won't be involved in the trial anymore. I was representing you, not her. I imagine she will have her own lawyer who will contact you." Lucy looked at me; I think her expression was relief. We could be together without me being in a lawyer capacity.

"Oh, well I owe you a dinner, then, to say thank you for everything you have done for us."

I didn't argue, but I imagined he would change his mind as soon as he was free. He was caught up in it all right now. I let Lucy and Anthony speak for a while before we decided we should head back to the police station. The two had a lot of things that needed working out. He had a lot of things to apologise for, but there was time for that later.

When we arrived, we were told that Vera would be here any minute and I felt nervous.

"Are you sure you want to be here?" I asked Lucy.

"I want to see her before she goes to prison," Lucy said bluntly. Before I could ask any more questions, Vera was walked in. She had a calm expression, but burst into tears as soon as she saw Lucy. That sadness quickly turned to anger when her eyes caught me.

"You stupid man!" she shouted out to me, making Lucy grab my hand. "Do you have any idea what you have done?" I didn't really understand what she meant, but I imagine she was just emotional.

"Do you think I did this because of an *affair*?" she continued.

Till Death Parts Us

Lucy looked quickly between the two of us.

"What do you mean?" she called towards her.

"There's another box. What I did was for the greater good."

My blood ran cold.

There was another box.

Fifty-Two

Lucy

James and I raced back to my parents' house and up to my father's office.

"Stay back there, Lucy," he said as he started trying to peel off the other floorboards around where he found the first box. It took a while, but eventually one came loose. My heart was pumping fast as I watched James pull a box out of it. Tentatively, he opened it and looked inside. I watched as his eyes widened at the sight, a painful expression on his face.

"What is it, James?" I asked, walking towards him.

"No, Lucy!" His shout made me jump. "Please, stay there."

I didn't listen and I approached the box. He tried to shut it, but I snatched a few photos out of his hand. What I saw were images that would haunt me for the rest of my life. The box was full of pictures of dead women who had clearly been beaten badly. They were barely recognisable. I ran to the bathroom as James called after me, retching in the toilet. I didn't return for a long time and he eventually knocked on the door. When I let him in, he pulled me into him. Neither of us really knew what to say in this moment.

Those pictures weren't just of women he was having an affair with.
These were his victims.
My father is a murderer.

Eventually, we went into my bedroom and sat down. James was clutching the box which he had now closed.

"Your mother told me she killed Amber for the greater good. I just thought she meant her own greater good, so that he wouldn't cheat on her again." He started crying. "I didn't realise…"

"How were you supposed to know?"

"If I had known, I never would have recorded that tape." He laid back on the bed. *The tape.* We had just sent my mother to prison for the rest of her life, all because she was trying to stop him from hurting more women over and over again.

"When the officer came, she kept saying *I knew it,* over and over again. At the time, I thought she was such a bitch." I laid down next to him. "She really did know it and she had tried to stop it."

"James, what are we going to do?" I couldn't undo what we had done already. The police had evidence and a verbal confession from my mother. There was no way they were going to release her now.

"I don't know," James said, his voice cold. "There's every chance they won't believe this was him. Given what your mother has admitted to doing, they could easily pin this all on her. It could get messy."

"Do we know for sure it was him?" Our eyes met. *We knew.*

Lucy

"These are violent killings, killings of the same women included in the first box. I think we both agreed the drugging and strangling wasn't your father's MO. Given the temper he showed me when I pushed him, I could see him doing this easily. Knowing he's guilty is one thing, proving it is another."

I suddenly felt helpless.

I had almost convinced myself before that it was okay that I had gotten my mother arrested because I would be getting my father back. Now, I am left with neither of my parents and images that I'll never get over. This happy family I was raised in was all a lie. Both my parents had kept secrets in their closets that were forcing their way out.

I was the daughter of not one, but *two* killers.

I was raised by monsters.

"We can't take this to the police, Lucy." I looked at James strangely. "I had a look through the rest of the photos when you were in the bathroom, your father isn't in any of the deceased's photos. There's no proof that he was there and we can't prove he knew them in the first place. All he needs is a good defence team and he will get away with it."

"If we take this to the police, they are going to blame my mother, aren't they?"

"Hell, hath no fury like a woman scorned." He sighed. "If she admitted to killing Amber because of the affair, they could assume she killed the rest of them, too. They heard her tell us about a box, meaning she knew where the photos were and did nothing. It only makes her look more guilty if we show them the box. We can't let this get out."

He stood up, pacing the room. "Even if we do convince them it was your father, it's going to be one hell of a battle. Something like this could go on for years. Everything will be completely turned upside down. You'll be put through more hell than you have already, Lucy."

"James I don't know if I can cope with a trial," He looked at me knowingly, that thought was already on his mind. Having to watch both my parents accusing each other of killings, the press following me around worse than now. Would there be more angry father's like Carter seeking revenge? "So, my dad just gets away with it?" I don't know if I could cope with both of my parents on trial, the messy investigation, my entire existence coming under scrutiny.

"I didn't say that," I could see his brain turning as he sat next to me.

"You have a plan?"

"I do. Maybe we need to take justice into our own hands."

Fifty-Three

James

Some people deserve to die.
If you had said that to me a week ago, I would have argued this point. I would tell you maybe people are capable of change, that they can be rehabilitated. That version of me is gone now and in this case, he deserves everything he has coming to him. Truthfully, I don't think death is enough of a punishment, but I don't know if I have it in me to make him suffer. *I'm not a monster*.

I've never killed anyone before and it was something I never thought I would or could do. I was doing this for Lucy, I was doing this for *us*. She had been through enough and these women had suffered at his hands. Sometimes justice needs to be taken into your own hands.

My eyes wander to the light in the kitchen as I approach the house, his outline coming into view. Washing up dishes seems like such a basic activity, like something any normal person would do. This wasn't a normal person and something about watching them made me uneasy. Was it exhausting to have to pretend all the time?

Making my way up to the door, I gently knocked, trying to make the sound of my fist on the door as non-threatening as possible. I don't know why I was so worried since I was an expected guest; my appearance was no surprise to him. The door swung open and I was greeted with a smile.

I never thought I'd feel this way, I am someone who puts justice above everything else. I now realise justice isn't always putting someone behind bars—sometimes you have to take justice into your own hands. Some crimes were punishable by death.

I tried to fight my own conflicted emotions.

This was different than what he did. His crimes were done out of evil; I am doing this for love. I am doing this to make sure no one else falls victim to those hands again.

The predator was about to become my prey.

I had been part of this world long enough to know he would never see prison time for what he did. I became suspicious whilst we were working the case that there was more going on. Maybe he was innocent of killing Amber, but there were other crimes he was guilty of. Other crimes he needed to be punished for.

When I opened that box, I realised what had been staring me in the face all along. Anthony Davis was a killer, just not of the person he was accused of. I felt guilty for turning Vera in; she had killed Amber in order to stop Anthony. She knew he was never going to get caught for his crimes, he was clearly careful in what he did. He had perfected it after all of these years. When I dug through further, the women appeared to

James

be from all different states.

That was what Vera was so desperate for Lucy to remember. She had forgotten that his career used to mean he travelled a lot for work. When the memories came flooding back, she recalled that they would always argue whenever he came back. She was too young to understand, but she thinks it had to be about the affairs.

The affairs that turned into murders.

Her mother had told her on the phone that they were safer with him then without him. She was aware of what he was capable of and didn't want them to fall on the wrong side of his temper. She was just a frightened woman trying to do the best for her kid.

Anthony hid it well, I had to give him credit. Regardless of the uneasy feeling he had always given me, he appeared to be a doting father. More than Vera, at least. That didn't change the fact he was prepared to abandon Lucy, as well, though. He was clearly capable of emotions, there was just a dark secret hidden behind him.

We placed the photos back under the floorboard before we left. Well, all of them except one. We didn't want him to get wind that we had found those ones, too, it would ruin the plan.

With Vera being charged, Anthony had been released and I had graciously accepted his dinner invite. Now, I felt nerves threatening to break me as I knocked on the door.

"Better late than never." He gave me a smirk as he opened the door.

"Sorry I'm late." I returned the smile as I entered the house. I had been sitting in the car round the corner just trying to convince myself I was doing the right thing.

"I did bring your favourite or so I'm told, anyway." I smiled wider as I held up the bottle of malbec in my hand. It was a struggle to hold polite conversation with him as anger boiled inside of me. Everything he did, everything he had put Lucy through.

"Oh, you know my poison. Red wine has a history of getting me into a lot of trouble over the years." A light chuckle followed. *It was about to again*, I thought to myself. "Can I interest you in a glass?" I shook my head.

"I'm driving, I need to keep a clear head." Besides, I prefer my wine *without* sleeping pills mixed in with it. "Just a soda for me, if you have it." My words were met with a nod as he moved towards the fridge. I watched as he poured my drink and then a glass of wine from the bottle for themselves. My entire body froze as I watched him bring the glass to his lips; I could feel my heart pounding in my chest. Suddenly, I felt panicked that he might be able to taste what I have done. I didn't need him to be completely asleep, I just needed his defences down. A little wooziness to make the whole thing easier.

My eyes wandered around the kitchen.

It was littered with photos, ranging from candid shots to staged photos. I wondered how it felt to live a lie, to hide who you truly were from all those that knew you. I can't even imagine waking up and finding out everything you know about the person you cared for was wrong. That the person you loved was a monster.

I guess if this didn't go my way, then people would be wondering that about me tomorrow. People I know waking up to the news that I killed someone. Details of my crimes plastered all over the newspaper. My family weeping in the living room as a police officer is telling them that the person

James

they knew was capable of heinous, wicked crimes. I hope it didn't come to that. I had worked out this plan in detail.

This was going to work.

Even if I got caught, I wouldn't be sorry. There would be no regret in my expression as I was dragged down to the station. Murder is evil, but sometimes it is necessary. The world will be a lot safer without him, I was certain of that. It was what encouraged me to be brave.

I struggled to take my eyes away from the photos as polite conversation continued. The usual talks about the weather and work ensued for a while. I turned my head, eyes now on the glass as more was poured. This was going to be easier than expected if he kept drinking like that.

"I'm thinking of trying that new restaurant downtown this week. Decent food has been missing from my life for a while." If only he knew he wouldn't be making that trip. This almost felt cruel—even death row inmates got a last meal. Maybe I should have brought something.

"It's supposed to be excellent," he continued. The slight slur on the last word caught my attention.

It's time.

"Did I tell you about—"

"We need to talk."

"Is that not exactly what we are doing?" I saw that anger I had seen from him before starting to bubble to the surface. The lion was going to show his teeth again.

"I know everything. Vera told me that whilst you may not have killed Amber, you are guilty of murder. You thought you'd be able to hide it from me?" I threw the picture I had taken out of the box on the table.

"It was an accident..." he said as if that made it better.

"It wasn't an accident and you know it. What about all the others?" I slammed my fist on the table. "We found your box of pictures upstairs. *Both boxes*. I know what you did to all of those women."

He at least had the decency to look guilty, his expression told me everything I needed to know. We had the right man.

"Wait. *We?*"

"Lucy and I. Your daughter knows everything you did." His face went pale. "I can't let you hurt anyone else, Anthony."

His eyes widened, panic creeping in. Before I allowed him to respond, I launched myself towards him, pressing him to the floor with my hands around his throat. There were attempts at thrashing, attempts to push me off, but they were futile. For once in my life, I felt like I had the upper hand. Slowly, Anthony's fight faded and I watched as his whole body went still underneath me. I waited a moment to be sure before moving myself off. I took a deep breath as I stood up and looked at what I had done.

My emotions were conflicted. On one hand, I know I have just saved more people from getting hurt by their hands. On the other hand, I have just made myself no better than them.

Some people deserved to die, I reminded myself.

Fifty-Four

Lucy

Never in my life would I have imagined myself going along with a plan like James had. As I listened to him, there wasn't a single part of me that disagreed with him. My father didn't deserve to live another day. He had destroyed the lives of all those women as well as my mother's. She would now spend the rest of her life in prison and those women would never get to have a future because of the things that he had done.

Some people deserved to die.

The only part of it that I didn't agree with was James doing it on his own. My father was a dangerous man, as he had clearly shown, and I was terrified that James would end up getting hurt. James refused to allow me to get into harm's way. He only agreed to do the plan if I waited in the car outside. He promised me he would be careful and not make any moves until the sleeping pills took effect.

Till Death Parts Us

Despite the fact neither of us had ever killed anyone before, I trusted him. James was the only person in the world who truly cared about me. He loved me so much he would kill for me if he had to .

And tonight, he was going to.

He parked me round the corner, he didn't want to risk any of the neighbours recognising his car. Nobody could know we were anywhere near here. James intended to make it look like the wine had been a gift from somebody, a welcome home from prison present. He came prepared with torn wrapping paper so it looked as if Anthony had opened it and immediately began drinking on his own. James would then make it look like there was a forced entry, that Anthony was taken by surprise. No trace that James had been there would be left.

I couldn't stop my knee from bouncing anxiously whilst I was waiting for James. Eventually, I saw him walk round the corner. He was keeping his pace calm, trying not to make himself seem suspicious.

There was one final part to our plan, the second box of photos. James placed it in the back seat as he climbed into the car.

"It's over, Lucy. He won't ever hurt anyone again." He turned the car on and started to pull away slowly.

My father was dead.

I should be crying, but no tears came. I had no tears to shed for a monster.

We arrived back at the cabin where Daines and Angie sat outside with Cato, a large campfire keeping them warm. They were our alibi. As far as anyone else was concerned, the four of us spent the night having a nice dinner together and sitting outside, enjoying the campfire together.

Lucy

James dumped the box of photos into the fire and we all sat in silence, watching them burn. My home would be crawling with police officers; we couldn't allow them to find this box of photos. There would be more questions than we could deal with. There was also a risk my mother would be blamed for their deaths; I couldn't put her through any more than she had already been through. If they found those photos, it also risked leading them to us. They knew James had found one box; we didn't want them to question him on a second. It was safer for everyone if we burned the evidence.

I watched as the last of the photos burned to ash. I hoped their souls were free now as the photos of their end no longer existed. I hoped they could rest in peace now that he was no longer on this Earth.

It was a long time before anybody spoke, the weight of what he, *we* had done lingered in the air. We were all an accessory to the crime, now. We were linked for life.

Tomorrow, a police officer would come and tell me my father was dead. I would crumble into James' arms, give my best fake cry, and pretend like I was grieving my father. I would put on a big show for them all and play the broken-hearted daughter.

The truth was, I don't think I was going to miss him. In these past couple of weeks, I had distanced myself from my parents. I had begun my new life and I needed to focus on that. I couldn't allow myself to dwell in the past or think about the ethics of everything that happened. We had to work out how to live with it now.

Hell hath no fury like a woman scorned, Dad.

Fifty-Five

James

One Year Later

I decided to take on Vera's case when it went to trial. I knew there was no hope of freeing her, but I wanted to make sure she got the best she could out of it. We decided to paint Anthony as the monster he was without exposing what we knew. Both Lucy and Vera testified that he was abusive towards them and had a violent history. I watched as they both took to the stands, stating the lies that I had taught them. We had practised it for weeks beforehand and they both gave a good show.

In a weird kind of way, I was proud of Lucy. I had always known she was brave, but seeing her strength through all of this blew me away. I was proud to be by her side. We played the angle that Vera had killed Amber to free herself from Anthony. That she was so desperate and it was the only

James

way out she could see. People bought it.

I read in the newspapers for weeks and could see that people felt sorry for Vera. They still wanted her held accountable, but she wasn't being trashed like Anthony was. When she was found guilty, she was still sentenced to life in prison, but in a minimum-security prison. She would have more privileges there and live better than she would at a maximum-security prison. It was the best I could do. It still didn't eradicate my guilt for the tape, but it helped.

We sold their family home as soon as we could after the investigation for Anthony ran cold. We didn't get much for it, but it was enough to buy us a small place in Rosehaven. We got the fresh start we both needed.

My relationship with my family was improving, I no longer felt like they were comparing me to Alice. We still struggled to speak about her still, but there was progress being made. It felt right to be in Rosehaven with Lucy. It felt exactly where I was supposed to be.

After everything went down, Michael Sawyer asked me to come back to the firm. *I refused.* I decided to start my own firm, do things my own way. I wanted to help people find justice for their family because they deserved it, not just for easy win cases. I had done a lot of bad things, but I hoped my work would help make up for my sins.

Sawyer lost the Murray case shortly after everything went down with Anthony.

Murray is appealing the decision, of course, but he's picked a different legal team this time. I will be representing him in his appeal next month.

But today isn't a day for me to be thinking about work, that can wait. Today is the day Lucy was going to become my wife. We wanted to ensure we were out of the woods with everything before we got married. It would seem suspicious to do something so joyous in a time of such darkness.

We were in the clear now; Anthony's case had gone cold and Vera's trial was over. It was time for the two of us to begin our lives together and I couldn't wait any longer to call Lucy my wife.

Fifty-Six

Lucy

Today felt bittersweet. On one hand, I was getting to marry the man I loved, but this day was not the way in which I had always dreamt it. I had always imagined my father walking me down the aisle and my mother spending the morning getting ready with me. Neither of them were here to see this day, but there is only one of them I would want to, anyway.

This past year has undoubtedly been the hardest year of my life. From having to play up my shock over my father's murder to having to stand at my mother's trial and act like he was an abusive father. I knew it was for the greater good, but it still made me sick to my stomach with all the lying. I wanted to be free from it, I wanted to move on.

We didn't have a normal proposal; it was more of a discussion. We both knew we wanted to get married, but we wanted the timing to be right. I asked him to wait until everything

Till Death Parts Us

had calmed down. I didn't want our marriage to begin in the middle of that chaos. I wanted us to move on and start again, closing the door on the past forever.

I will still speak and see my mother, but for my own sanity, I needed to move away.

It felt strange to be staring at myself in a wedding dress. I felt beautiful in it, but I knew James would think I was beautiful in anything. It was one of the reasons I loved him so much.

"God, you're gorgeous," Angie said as she helped me sort out my dress. She had been the most loyal friend I had, well her and Daines. The two of them had been our rocks throughout all of this. Nothing we ever asked them would be too much. We would all take what happened that night to our graves.

"Do you think he'll like it?"

"Oh, James won't know what to do with himself when he sees you." She laughed. "Ready?"

A year ago, I couldn't picture feeling happy again, but James helped me get here. He was by my side every single day, his love for me never faltered. We made our way to the church and I felt completely and utterly calm. We decided to keep it small, neither of us wanted the attention.

As I walked down the aisle, our eyes were locked on each other. It felt like no one else was in the room. Even as we went through the service, I could only focus on him. He was the person who always kept me on my feet during a storm.

When we were announced man and wife, he kissed me like he was scared he was going to lose me. There was an urgency to it and I was completely encapsulated by him. Cheers rang out as we walked back down the aisle and I saw his parents with Daines and Angie, alongside a few others we invited. This was a day filled with joy.

Lucy

"Ready to dance with me, Weatherston?" I teased as we made our way into the reception.

"I will always be ready to dance with you, boss." He smiled as he took me in his arms. We didn't leave each other's side for the whole evening. As the last song of the night played, he brushed my hair from my face and kissed me.

"God, I hope I go first," he said with a sad smile. "Because I couldn't live a day without you, Lucy *Weatherston,*" he said, emphasising my new last name as he spoke.

I don't know if I could ever live without him, either.

Fifty-Seven

James

Seventeen Years Later

My whole body was beaten down as I walked through the front door of my house. I stayed in the entrance for a while, just listening to the chatter of Lucy and our three children around the dinner table. *I'd missed this noise.* I was late. I always seem to be late for dinner these days. After a long day, there was nothing that I looked forward to more than a home cooked dinner by Lucy and hearing all about my family's day. Even as they started to become teenagers and the rebellion kicked in, we still had dinner. Lucy said her family would always be eating dinner together and she meant it.

"Dad!" My youngest, Lucas, was the first to greet me as I walked in. I gave him a hug before he returned to his seat. I mouthed *I'm sorry* to Lucy for what was the fourth time this week. Her face was sullen and I had a feeling it wasn't just because I was late. As I walked round my seat, I ruffled my eldest, Elijah's, hair. He was fifteen now, which was the age I was when Alice and I had gotten into the crash that took her life. That death changed me and took away what had been left of my childhood, of my happiness. I hoped my son never had to experience anything like that. I wanted all my kids to have the life that I never did.

"I hope you all have thanked your mother for cooking for you," I said as I sat down. A mixture of yes and a belated thank you played out between the three of them.

My eyes fell next to my daughter, Alice. Her resemblance to my sister was uncanny. She had Lucy's hair, but her features were all my sister's. Sometimes it was like her ghost was in the room with us. It was bittersweet watching her grow, knowing that one day I would watch her grow older than my sister ever got to be. I knew I needed to separate the two in my mind, but sometimes it was hard. I didn't want Alice to grow up and think she needed to be anyone other than herself. My little girl had her own mind and heart. I wanted her to follow those as she grew.

I sat in my chair, taking them all in. I listened to Elijah tell me about his classes, Alice about the book she was reading, and Lucas about some prank he pulled on his friends. For a moment, I forgot all about the stress of my job and my current case. I just let myself be in the moment, I never wanted my kids to feel like I was absent. When I was at home, they had my full attention, as did Lucy.

I looked over to my beautiful wife, but her attention was on the kids, too. I remembered how nervous I was when Lucy found out she was pregnant with Elijah. I knew she would be an incredible mother, but I wasn't sure what kind of father

Till Death Parts Us

I would be. I had done some bad things in my life, but these three kids, aside from marrying my wife, were the best thing I ever did. I couldn't be prouder of the life we have built together.

I had never put any pressure on Lucy to work. My salary as a lawyer meant we lived comfortably. She enjoyed spending her time volunteering as much as possible. I often wondered if she was trying to repent for what we did, *what I did*. Truthfully, I think she would have done this, regardless. Her face lit up when she spoke about some of the kids she tutored today.

It made me happy to see her smile, her beauty only grew as she got older. Meanwhile, I felt like I was starting to look like a tired, old man. I was pushing my body further than it could go and I knew that. I was so close to prosecuting one of the highest gang members in the city. I had worked countless hours to get here. Everything I had done, the bad and the good, was to get justice for those who deserved it. These gangs had left countless broken lives in their wake and it was time for them to get what they deserved. This was what everything I had ever done was about.

As we finished our meal, I nudged Elijah to help me clear up the table.

"Why don't you kids go watch some TV? I need to talk to your mother." They didn't need to be told twice as they all raced to the living room.

"You know, they are just going to fight over what to watch," Lucy said, crossing her arms.

"It keeps them out of our hair for a minute," I said as I made my way across the room to her, embracing her.

"More came today, James," she said quietly into my chest. I knew from her face when I came in that was what she was

James

going to say. She moved away from me and grabbed a stack of letters off the side.

As she opened the first letter, I saw the large words on the top.

We know what you did.

It wasn't the first time I had read those words, but my stomach dropped every time. Since I took on the case, they have been coming almost daily. At first, they just asked me to drop it and then they started ramping up, threats against me came thick and fast. I shuffled through the letters.

Drop the case or you will be the one who needs a lawyer.

It was the last one, however, that made my hands shake.

R.I.P Anthony Davis

As I looked up, I saw tears forming in my wife's eyes. "James, you need to drop the case, please."

I felt conflicted. There was no way they actually had proof of what I did. How could they? That was eighteen years ago. They had to be making assumptions. I was so careful back then.

"They won't have any proof, Lucy. These are just scare tactics."

"James…" She shook her head at me. "Is it worth the risk? Are you willing to risk losing us?" Lucy and I had this conversation many times over the last few weeks. Every time I tried to reassure her that nothing would happen. Now, as I saw her father's name on the letter, I knew I wouldn't be able to reassure her this time. This had gone on long enough.

"I would never risk losing you, boss." A small smile hit her lips as she unfolded her arms and allowed me to hold her close again. "I need a couple days to hand it over and then I'll drop the case, *I promise.*"

"Thank you." Standing on her tiptoes, she touched her lips to mine. It didn't matter how many years passed, my obsession with Lucy never faltered. Every time we parted, I always had a burning desire, a need for another kiss.

"Everything will be fine, Lucy. I'll always keep you and the kids safe. No matter what."

Fifty-Eight

Lucy

These letters had been coming through our door for weeks. I had been begging James to drop it. I'd even asked Daines to talk to him, but it made no difference. James was a stubborn man when he wanted to be. It wasn't until my father's name was mentioned that he listened. I don't know how, but somebody knew what we did all those years ago. It was too much of a coincidence for it to be somebody just trying to scare us.

I was grateful when he said he would drop it. It wasn't just the two of us to think about anymore. We had three children who were relying on us. If this got out, they would lose us. I couldn't let that happen.

I managed to fall asleep for the first time in weeks without the anxiety of these letters hanging over me. James was going to drop the case at the end of the week and this was all going to blow over.

Till Death Parts Us

We would go back to being a normal family. Everything was going to be okay.

I woke up to the sound of a bedroom door slamming coming from Elijah's room. Shifting out of bed, I followed just behind him down the stairs. As I reached the bottom of the stairs, my mouth dropped in shock. A man was pointing a gun directly at my husband and my eldest son. I stood frozen, unsure of what to do in this situation.

James was talking to the man calmly, offering him money if he left us alone. Something about this didn't feel right. The letters came to my head once more. *He's going to drop the case*, I wanted to scream out, but nothing came. Everything felt like it was moving in slow motion as Elijah ran off to get the money from his father's desk. When he returned, the man smacked Elijah, causing James to cry out defensively. Before I could register what was happening, a gun shot rang out.

"James*!*" I screamed. The gunshot still rang in my ears as I began to rush over to him. The man ran out the door with Elijah following quickly behind him.

"Elijah!" I shouted after him "Elijah, stop!" But he didn't. He was out of my sight, running fast after the shooter. I was torn between running after my son and helping James.

I needed to stop the bleeding, I needed to keep James alive. I pushed hard against the wound, my hands instantly becoming covered in his blood. The feeling made me feel sick, but I needed to be strong for him. He needed me now more than he ever had before. If roles were reversed, he wouldn't be panicking, he would know exactly what to do.

Would he have gone after Elijah? I really didn't know. I had no idea if I was making the correct choice. I could potentially lose two of my boys in one night. All because of that stupid

Lucy

case.

"James, I need you to keep your eyes open for me, okay?" I didn't know what else to say, I just kept my hands on the wound. Tears falling down my cheeks as I hoped help was on its way. It wasn't supposed to end like this.

Fifty-Nine

James

How is it possible that so much could be happening in the room around me, but everything was going so slowly? The paramedics and officers were all rushing around, but all I could see was *her*. *My Lucy*. Her hand clutched onto mine as she spoke to me. I tried to focus on her words, but I felt myself fading in and out. I wanted to hear her voice so I strained to listen.

I needed to hear her voice.

"James, everything is going to be okay, I promise." Her soft voice finally filled my ears. Willing me to keep my eyes open. When I first met her, I believed her when she told me she thought her father was innocent. I always had a way of telling whether or not she was telling the truth. Which is why even now, in my weak state, she was lying to me.

Everything was not going to be okay.

I'm going to die.

James

I could feel it inside me as my body began to shut down. I was getting weaker with each second that passed. I kept my eyes locked on Lucy's face, I wanted her to be the last thing I ever saw. She had been my reason for living for so long and I didn't want to forget her in death. I wanted to carry her image through with me until the day she joined me. As much as I would miss her, I hope the day she joined me was not for a long time. She deserved to live a long life, to be happy. She was an incredible mother to our children and they needed her. They would all be okay without me as long as they had her. Lucy was a beacon of light to every body around her and I was so lucky to have loved her for so long.

I would wait as long as it took to see her again.

I wasn't afraid of death, but I was afraid of leaving Lucy and my kids behind. I wondered if this was my karma for killing Anthony all those years ago. If I'd only ever gotten one minute with Lucy in my life, I still wouldn't have changed a thing. Some people deserved to die and I guessed today that was me.

I deserved this.

My eyes briefly left hers as Daines walked into the room. I don't even think he is on duty tonight, but I guess someone called him.

"James…" His voice shook. He stood across the room like a frightened child, like he was afraid to come too close to me. I had never seen such weakness in my friend and I ached for him. Was it strange that even in my state, I wanted to reach out to him, to tell him everything was going to be okay? That everyone would be okay without me.

I knew Daines would protect my family the way he had always protected me, and I him. We were brothers not by blood, but in every other way that is counted. If roles were reversed, I would do whatever it took to take care of his wife, Angie. My family was safe in his hands.

Before Daines could respond, I noticed Elijah run back into the room, kneeling down next to me. I felt him take my other hand. A weak smile crossed my lips. Surrounded by those I loved was not a bad way to go. These people around me and my other two children were my legacy and I was proud of it.

"You're not allowed to leave me. You know that, don't you?" Lucy's voice found its way to me again. My chest ached to see her in pain. "You promised me we'd spend our retirement driving the RV round the country." I felt as if another bullet had landed in my chest at her words. There were so many things I had wanted us to do together that would no longer happen now. I hoped Lucy still did all of those things, I hoped she never stopped living.

"Do you remember what I told you when we got married?" I was beginning to struggle to speak, my eyes fluttered slightly as I gathered the strength to continue.

"I told you I hoped I went before you." A cough interrupted me. "Because I couldn't live a day without you, Lucy."

I meant it when I said it back then and I meant it now. I could not live a day without her. I wouldn't know how to survive without her, I don't think I could do it. She was different. Lucy was strong and she was brave. I was proud to call her my wife, she would be okay.

"Not yet, please." I heard her beg me, but I no longer had the energy to respond. I struggled to keep my eyes open as I gazed at her, it was my time now.

I love you, Lucy Weatherston. I will find you in every lifetime.

Sixty

Lucy

Fifteen Years Later

Every Monday like clockwork you will find me at James' grave. We met on a Monday and he died on a Monday. It feels like a full circle to be here each week. Occasionally over the years, I have been away or unavailable, but I still thought of him. I still spent that time on a Monday morning thinking of nothing else but James.

This particular Monday felt sadder than most; it is approaching sixteen years since his death now. Not only that, but our eldest, Elijah, got married the previous weekend. It was another big event that James didn't get to see. I had witnessed graduations, the birth of our granddaughter, Violet, and our new grandson and daughter-in-law coming into the family without him by my side. Despite her recent divorce, he missed walking our daughter, Alice, down the aisle. I know he would have been the shoulder to cry on that she needed when it all fell apart. I never quite found the right words to comfort her, but I know he would have. He would absolutely have loved working on cars with Lucas and the fact his old truck was still being driven around. James would have savoured every single moment with us and it tore me apart that the opportunity was taken away from him.

Tears formed in my eyes as I made my way down the familiar path of the cemetery. I felt close to him when I was here. For a minute, I would almost forget he was gone. As I approached, I took in the plants around the grave—Alice had always helped me keep the area nice for him. I took a seat on the bench opposite.

"We had your picture with us on Saturday," I began to tell him. I know it may seem strange to talk out loud, especially since he couldn't talk back, but I found comfort in it over the years. I had already told him all about Elijah's wife, Lottie, and her son, Theo. He would have absolutely loved them, there was no doubt in my mind. James would be out on that boat, taking Theo and Violet fishing at the earliest opportunity just like he did for our kids. "It was Lottie's idea, actually. We all had lockets with your picture and the boys had a copy in their jackets. We thought it would help you be with us on the day, make sure you didn't miss a thing." I let out a soft sigh. "I definitely felt you there, I know you would have been the first one on that dance floor with me, Weatherston."

My mind went back to one of the first nights we went dancing together at Pegasus. It was the first time James told me he loved me. We went back to that place many times before it eventually shut down, but I will always remember that night. It was the night I knew I was his and he was mine.

Lucy

It was always one of my favourite things we did, dancing. Every summer, we went to the gala in Rosehaven together, even after the kids were born. It was like a ritual to dance the night away together. The gala still goes on, but I stopped going when James passed.

I didn't feel like dancing anymore without him.

I try to show up as much as possible for my kids. I don't let them see how much I am hurting. Without their father, I knew I needed to be strong for them. I was lucky in having Daines and Angie, although she passed a few years after James. They helped massively especially in the early days. When I felt like I couldn't get out of bed, they were there. My house was always clean and food was always in the fridge. Even to this day, I know Daines watches out for all the kids, especially Elijah. The two work together on the force and watching them is like watching James and Daines thirty years ago. Instantly, I am thrown back in time, watching the love and banter around me. James would love how close they are.

"I see you every day through our kids." I allowed the tears to fall as I fiddled with my dress. "I see you in Elijah's smile, Alice's eyes, and Lucas' laugh. All three of them carry around my favourite part of you." A smile graced my lips. "They have your kind heart, James. Your selfless nature. That desire you always had to help everyone around you." I wiped my face with my sleeve.

"Oh, James, how proud you would be if you could see them now. I often can't believe three beautiful souls came from me considering where I came from." I shook memories of my parents from my brain as soon as they arrived. They did not deserve to be a part of my life; they did not deserve to consume my thoughts.

I survived that part of my life; James *saved* me from that life. We did things that we carried with us, but I wouldn't take it back. I don't regret my part in my father's death or in putting my mother in prison. They deserved everything that came their way. My only regret in life is not stopping James from working the gang case which caused his murder.

I tried to make him stop, to drop the case sooner. I know Daines tried, too.

One of James' best traits was also his downfall. He was determined to help everybody around him. It was what I loved most about him, and in the end, it was the reason he was taken from me.

When it first happened, I was too overwhelmed with grief and raising my children to focus on what happened. As time went on, I struggled with that niggling feeling that those responsible for James' death were still out there. If the roles were reversed, he would have immediately hunted them down and destroyed them.

There was a sense of guilt that consumed me that I had not yet done the same for him.

I don't think I will ever be at peace until he is avenged. I don't care how long it takes; they were going to pay for what they did to James. Even if it was the last thing I ever did.

"I'll do whatever it takes, James. I won't let you down." With those words I picked myself up and headed home.

I had work to do.

Don't worry, Lucy's story isn't over yet.

Acknowledgments

To everyone who has taken the time to read James and Lucy's story thank you. When I wrote the prologue of my first book Read My Rights I knew I wanted to write their story. No love story lasts forever but that doesn't mean the journey isn't worth telling.

A key theme within this book is that of unconditional love which brings me nicely into my next thank you.

To Tom, you may not be out there thwarting my enemies like James (which is probably not a bad thing as I don't think an orange jumpsuit would be your colour either) but I know you will always have my back. I hope we find each other in every lifetime.

To Alessia, I have many things to thank you for. Firstly for the cover of this book, I wanted you to take creative control because I knew you'd kill it and you did. Thank you for bringing them to life. I also want to thank you for your endless support. You have spent this past year listening to my endless voice notes and messages, I will always be grateful to you and everything you have done.

To my editor Hannah, this story would not be what it is without you. We are team when it comes to this author malarkey and in my opinion a pretty good one at that. Thank you always.

To my Street Team/ARC Readers, you are a vital part of the publishing process and I appreciate you taking the chance and helping me on this journey.

To all those who have gone from strangers, to friends and now are like family. Thank you for always holding me up.

Also by Caz Redpath

Read My Rights
You only have one chance to make a good first impression.

Haunted by his father's murder, Elijah is desperate to control every element of his life. A failure to make an arrest on duty leaves him in a foul mood. Later that day as a vehicle fails to stop his anger hits boiling point, with the driver in the firing line.

Charlotte is trying to make a fresh start with her young son in a new town, but a heated discussion with a local officer threatens to derail everything. She tries to move ahead with her new life hoping the two won't cross paths again. Little does she know that giving a second chance on a first impression might just save her life.

Printed in Great Britain
by Amazon